Captain Sisko . . . in His Own Words!

" 'Captain?' Major Kira said to me as her face appeared on the *Defiant*'s viewscreen. 'Where were you? We were . . .'

" 'Major,' I said, 'you have exactly thirty seconds before an attack on the station. Go to red alert. The first sign of the attack will be dizziness, then a hundred or so armed troops will beam into the station even though the screens are up. If you can't hold Ops, disable anything you can, especially shields and weapons. Do you understand?'

" 'Aye, sir,' Kira said, and before I could close the comm link she had already turned to issue orders to defend my station against invaders from the Mist. . . .''

STAR TREK

DEEP SPACE NINE®

THE CAPTAIN'S TABLE

BOOK THREE OF SIX

THE MIST

BENJAMIN SISKO

AS RECORDED BY
DEAN WESLEY
SMITH

AND
KRISTINE KATHRYN
RUSCH

THE CAPTAIN'S TABLE CONCEPT BY
JOHN J. ORDOVER AND DEAN WESLEY SMITH

POCKET BOOKS

New York   London   Toronto   Sydney   Tokyo   Singapore

An *Original* Publication of POCKET BOOKS

POCKET BOOKS, a division of Simon & Schuster Inc.
1230 Avenue of the Americas, New York, NY 10020

ISBN: 0-671-01471-4

First Pocket Books printing July 1998

10 9 8 7 6 5 4 3 2 1

For Mark and Laura Nelson

THE MIST

CHAPTER

1

ON A VAST FRONT spread through the Alpha Quadrant, the battle between the Federation and Dominion waged on, ship by ship, sector by sector. Moving through an unusually empty section of space near the Klingon/Federation border, three Jem'Hadar ships raced to reinforce four other Dominion ships in a losing fight against the Federation starship *Defiant* and the Klingon battle cruiser *Hutlh*.

Without warning, and directly in front of the three Jem'Hadar reinforcements, a white line formed in the blackness of space, slowly filling into a large area of mist, as if it were a cloud building before a storm. It had no substance that registered on any instrument, and the three ships entered it, expecting their shields to protect them against the thin anomaly. They were within two minutes of the fight and they had no time to detour around a simple cloud of space debris.

But no ships reappeared on the other side of the thin area of mist.

A few moments later the mist faded and was gone, as quickly as it had come, leaving the space empty and black.

No Jem'Hadar reinforcements arrived at the battle, and the Federation starship *Defiant* and the Klingon battle cruiser *Hutlh* fought and destroyed the four Dominion ships, holding the line of the war for one more day.

The disappearance of the three Jem'Hadar reinforcement ships became an unexplained footnote in the records of a long and deadly war.

But sometimes wars are won in the footnotes.

The cool metal handle on the massive wooden door fit into Captain Benjamin Sisko's hand as if it were made for him. The feeling so startled him that he paused and glanced down, opening his hand without taking his fingers off the metal.

The handle's design was Bajoran, shaped almost like another hand reaching out, yet without the delineation of a hand or fingers. It was clearly very old and very well made. The surface was worn smooth, polished by use. Sisko couldn't see anything that attached the handle to the door, almost as if the handle grew from the dark wood.

Above Sisko's head was a carved wooden sign that read simply, THE CAPTAIN'S TABLE. The sign was an extension of the doorframe and the letters on the sign were dried and cracked, obviously from the heat of the Bajoran summers. Yet the sign, along with the door and the griplike handle, seemed to reach out to Sisko and pull him in, welcoming him as if he were coming back to a childhood home.

A few weeks before, a captain of a Jibetian freighter had pulled Sisko aside on the Promenade and asked if he knew where a bar called the Captain's Table might be. Sisko had said he'd never heard of the place. Instead, he recommended Quark's.

The Jibetian had simply laughed and said, "If you ever get the chance, have a drink in the Captain's Table. There is no other bar."

Sisko had put the man's suggestion out of his mind until this morning. He was on Bajor because Dr. Bashir had threatened to have Sisko relieved of command if he did not rest. It was impossible to rest in the middle of a war, Sisko had argued, but Bashir was adamant. A Starfleet doctor did have the power to relieve someone of command, and rather than go through that fight, Sisko had agreed to two days on Bajor, two days without meetings, without Starfleet protocol, without decisions.

If he had stayed on the station, he wouldn't have been able to relax. Somehow the staff seemed to believe that Sisko had to decide which replicators remained on-line, which messages should be forwarded through the war zone, which ships would be allowed to dock. He had a competent crew; it was time, Bashir had said, to trust them with the details, and to sleep.

Bashir had wanted Sisko on Bajor for a week. Sisko

3

DEAN W. SMITH & KRISTINE K. RUSCH

wanted to stay overnight, and return in less than twenty-four hours. They had compromised on two days.

"Two *full* days," Bashir had said. "If I hear of you on this station before forty-eight hours are up, I will order you to the infirmary for the remainder of your holiday."

"I'll keep that in mind," Sisko had said, deciding that he'd rather remain on Bajor than subject himself to sickbay for even one hour. Bashir had smiled, knowing that he'd won.

Sisko spent his first day on Bajor in his rented cabin, sitting outside and wondering what the planet would be like when he retired there. If he got a chance to retire there.

By that afternoon, he was restless—despite Bashir's worry, Sisko had too much energy to relax. His concerns for the Federation, for the entire quadrant, would not allow him to rest. Not completely. And no matter how much he loved Bajor, it didn't take his mind off the problems he would face when he returned.

He wandered the streets of the nearby village, and had passed this very door more than once. On his third pass, the sign had caught his attention and the Jibetian captain's words had come back to him. Sisko had had his fingers wrapped around the handle before he'd even realized that he'd made a decision.

The door was so massive-looking that Sisko expected it to feel heavy as he pulled it open. Instead it moved easily, almost as if it had no weight at all.

Inside, the coolness and darkness gripped him, pulling him out of the heat of the Bajoran day. Instantly he could feel the sweat on his forehead, where moments before the dryness of the afternoon air had pulled it instantly away. He let the door swing shut slowly behind him, seeming to plunge him into complete darkness. His eyes struggled to adjust from the bright sunlight to the dim light. The coolness now wrapped completely around him like a welcome hand. In the cool air, he was suddenly more thirsty than normal.

Part of his thirst came from the smell. The interior had a soft scent, like the smell of fresh-baked bread long after it had been eaten. Or the scent of coffee just percolating in the morning. Familiar smells. Welcoming smells. Smells that made him think of comfort and of home.

He stood still, with his back to the door, and dim shapes appeared as his eyes adjusted.

Walls.

Pictures on the walls.

Soon he could tell that he was in a short hallway fashioned out of smooth wood and decorated with images of old water-sailing ships. Only a single indirect light above the ceiling illuminated the small passage. Deeper inside he could hear talking and an occasional laugh. He stepped forward and around a corner.

In front of him was a large yet comfortable-feeling room. The ceiling was low and a stone fireplace filled part of the wall to his left, a small fire doing nothing to take the comfortable coolness from the room. Most of the right wall of the room was filled with a long wooden bar fronted by a dozen or more stools. The surface of the bar looked worn and well used. A tall, thick man stood behind the bar, and at least a dozen patrons from different races sat around some of the tables in small groups.

Sisko stopped in the entrance, giving his eyes time to finish adjusting to the dim light. It was then that he noticed the grand-style piano in the corner to his left. It seemed old and very well used, its surface marred by what looked like hundreds of glass and bottle imprints.

Beside the piano a humanoid sat. He was from no race that Sisko recognized. The humanoid had slits for eyes, lizardlike skin, and four long talons on each hand. Sisko felt no fear or revulsion, but merely a sense of curiosity and a feeling of comfort coming from the creature.

"Welcome, Captain," the large man behind the bar said, smiling and motioning Sisko forward. With one more glance at the unmoving humanoid, Sisko turned and stepped toward the bar.

The bartender wore a white apron with an open-necked gray shirt under it. He had unruly white hair and a smile that seemed to take the dimness out of the air. Sisko liked the man instantly, not exactly knowing why, and not willing to explore why. Sisko was on vacation. It was time he relaxed. He usually knew better than to be lulled into a feeling of safety, and yet here he was. He was conscious of his back, conscious of the people around him, but he wasn't really wary. Not yet. And he wouldn't be unless something made him feel that way.

Sisko stepped between two of the bar stools. To his surprise, he had to look up to meet the gaze of the man behind the bar.

"They call me Cap," the bartender said in a deep, rich voice that seemed to have a touch of laughter floating through it. "Welcome to the Captain's Table. What's your drink of choice?" He wiped his hands on a bar rag, and then waited.

Sisko glanced down the long back bar filled with glasses of all shapes and sizes. Above the glasses were what seemed like hundreds of different bottles of liquor. He couldn't spot a replicator. He had a thousand choices, but at the moment he wanted something to take away the last of the Bajoran heat and dryness.

"Do you have Jibetian ale?"

Cap laughed and nodded. "You'll have to go a great deal more than that to stump this place. We have just about everything. Would you like your ale warm, cold, or lightly salted?"

Sisko had never liked the Jibetian habit of salting their ale. "Cold," he said. "No salt."

Betraying a lightness on his feet that didn't seem natural to a man his size, Cap spun and opened up a cooler under the back bar. A moment later he slid a cold, damp bottle of Jibetian ale into Sisko's hand.

"Thanks," Sisko said, tilting the bottle toward Cap in a small, appreciative salute.

Jibetian ale was the perfect drink for Sisko's mood.

It was hard to come by, almost impossible since the start of the war with the Dominion. Quark claimed to have one bottle left in his stock, and the price he placed on it made it seem as if it were the last bottle anywhere in the universe. Sisko had thought he would have to forgo Jibetian ale until the Federation defeated the Dominion.

Almost as if he had read Sisko's mind, Cap said, "I think I got a few more where that came from."

"Excellent," Sisko said. "I wish I had time for more than one."

Cap just smiled as if what Sisko had said had amused him. Then the bartender turned back to cleaning glasses.

Sisko watched him for a moment, then took a drink. The rich, golden taste of the ale relaxed him, draining some of the problems he carried, almost as if they didn't exist. He downed half the bottle before finally forcing himself to stop for a breath. He very seldom drank, so going too fast wasn't the best idea, no matter how good it tasted. And this was real ale, not synthehol. Its effects would be real as well.

Cap was still washing glasses, so Sisko turned and studied the bar. He had half expected, in the middle of the afternoon, to be the only one inside. But that clearly wasn't the case. Five of the ten tables had groups at them, the sounds of their talking filling the low-ceilinged bar with a full background sound. If Sisko focused, he could hear individual conversations, but overall the noise level was not too loud.

The patrons of this bar were an odd mix. A number

of humans, a young, almost childlike man from a race Sisko couldn't identify, and a half-dozen other races he had seen on the station. He would have thought this mix normal at Quark's, which had the entire quadrant to draw on. Here, in a small out-of-the-way bar on Bajor, the mix was odd indeed, especially since there were no Bajorans present.

A huge Caxtonian sat at the opposite end of the bar, nursing a drink. The Caxtonian looked as if he never left that stool, which struck Sisko. He had never heard of a Caxtonian ever visiting Bajor. There were a number of strange things about this place, and yet, he still didn't feel uncomfortable. Perhaps that was the strangest of all. He had been on alert ever since the threat to the Alpha Quadrant began; he'd thought he wouldn't relax until the situation was resolved.

Perhaps Bashir was right. Perhaps Sisko had needed this.

He had finished off another quarter of the bottle and was about to ask Cap about some of the customers when behind him a loud, grating voice boomed over the background talking.

"Sisko! You are a long way from your precious station."

As Sisko turned, the mostly empty ale bottle in his hand, he noticed that Cap wasn't smiling quite as much as he had been a moment before.

"I could say the same for you, Sotugh," Sisko said, turning to face the Klingon who stood near a table on the far side of the room. Sisko hadn't seen him a moment before, yet he knew that voice without even seeing its owner. And now he was even more surprised at the patrons of this bar.

Sotugh, head of the House of DachoH, commanded a large percentage of the Klingon fleet under Gowron. He was loyal to the Empire almost to a fault, and made clear his disgust at the current alliance between the Federation and the Klingon Empire against the Dominion. Yet he had fought many brilliant battles in the course of the war. The last time Sisko had heard, Sotugh and his ships were patrolling a sector of the Cardassian border.

"Bah," Sotugh said, waving his hand in disgust at Sisko's comment. He was a large man, even for a Klingon. His graying hair flowed over his clothing which, surprisingly, was not his uniform. Sisko wasn't sure if he'd ever seen Sotugh out of uniform before.

"Gentlemen," Cap said, his voice stopping Sotugh from continuing. "Instead of yelling across the bar, I suggest you sit down together and continue this conversation."

"Sit with Sisko," Sotugh said, laughing at the suggestion of the bartender. "I will fight with him against the Dominion, but nothing more."

Sisko leaned over his ale. "Still mad at me for the Mist incident, I see."

Sotugh's hand went to his knife. "The Mist would be members of the Empire if not for your action. Their weapons would help us fight the Cardassian and Dominion scum."

Sisko smiled. "As usual," he said deliberately, "your opinions blind you, Sotugh."

Sotugh stepped forward, his hand gripping his knife.

"Sotugh!" Cap said, his voice stopping the Klingon warrior in midstep. "Only a coward draws on an unarmed man. You are not known as a coward."

Sisko placed the bottle on the bar and opened both his hands to show Sotugh that they were empty. The bartender clearly knew how to handle Klingons. Around the bar a few other patrons laughed softly.

Sotugh only looked angry, but his hand left his knife.

"It seems," Cap said, "that since the Mist are considered nothing but legend, there is a story behind this. Am I right, Captain?"

Sisko picked up his bottle and finished the last of the ale. "There is a story," he said. He grinned at Sotugh, who only sneered in return. All the patrons in the bar now had their attention riveted on the two.

While the tension held the bar in silence, Cap opened another bottle of Jibetian ale and slid it down the bar, stopping it just beside Sisko's hand. Then he quickly poured what looked like a mug of blood wine. "Arthur, hand this to Sotugh."

The young-looking alien, the one who looked like a slender child, grabbed the mug from the bar. He moved easily across the floor, his robes flowing around him, and handed the mug to Sotugh as if the glowering Klingon were nothing more than a happy patron.

"I would be very interested in hearing a story about the Mist," Cap said. "Would anyone else?"

It seemed that from the yesses and applause, every-one agreed. Sisko only shook his head in amusement at Sotugh's expression of disgust. It had been a number of years since the meeting with Sotugh over the race called the Mist. There was nothing secret about the incident. But it hadn't become widely known, since shortly after it happened the Klingons invaded Cardassia. Now the story would only add to the legend of the Mist.

"Pull a couple of those tables together," Cap said, pointing at a few tables in the center of the room. "Does anyone need refills before the story starts?"

The young Arthur took Sotugh's blood wine before the Klingon had a chance to drink and set the mug on an empty table. To Sisko's surprise, Sotugh did not seem to mind. He went to the nearest chair, chased away a yellow-and-green gecko with a stumpy tail, grabbed his mug, and took a long drink, slopping some of the liquid down the side. Miraculously, Arthur managed to avoid getting drops on his robe.

Two patrons quickly pulled another table over to Sotugh's. Sisko nodded to Cap and moved over to the group table, sitting across from the Klingon. After a moment everyone in the bar, except for the Caxtoni-an at the bar and the strange lizard-man near the door, had gathered at the large table with drinks in their hands.

"Sotugh," Sisko said, smiling at his old adversary. "Would you like to start? Klingons are legendary for their ability to tell a story."

Sotugh simply waved his hand in disgust. "Klingons tell stories of honor. But this story has no honor for anyone. You tell it. I will correct your errors."

Sisko took a quick sip from the bottle of cold ale, then nodded at Cap, who stood near the bar.

"In my years in Starfleet, I have seen many strange things," Sisko said. "But little as strange as the Mist."

"Now that," Sotugh said, "is something I agree with."

Sisko smiled at Sotugh. He had known it would be impossible for the Klingon to keep silent during this story.

Cap laughed. "Sotugh, you have given the story over to Captain Sisko. Please let him tell it."

Sotugh sat back in disgust, the mug of blood wine clutched in his hands.

"Go ahead, Captain," Cap said.

"As you may have gathered, most of this story will be hard to believe. But I'm sure Sotugh will correct anything I may get wrong."

Sotugh only grunted.

"I first heard the legend of the Mist," Sisko said, "when I was a cadet in Starfleet Academy, but I didn't encounter them until many years later. By then I had almost forgotten who and what they were. . . ."

CHAPTER
2

MY CONTACT WITH the Mist occurred during the period of tension between the Klingon Empire and the Federation, just before this quadrant's problems with the Dominion began. For those of you who do not know, I command *Deep Space Nine,* a former Cardassian space station, one of the farthest outposts of the Federation. We are the guardians of the wormhole between the Alpha and Delta Quadrants.

We run a twenty-four-hour clock on *Deep Space Nine,* following the long-standing Federation tradition of maintaining an Earth Day in space. I am in my office—which used to be the Cardassian commander Gul Dukat's office—in Operations by 0800 hours, and my staff knows not to disturb me until I have finished my first and only glass of *raktajino.* It is not that I awaken slowly, or even in a bad mood. I simply prefer a few moments of silence at the beginning of my day, since I know that, if the day runs true to form, those will be the only moments of silence I will have.

So that morning, when my first officer, Major Kira, our liaison with Bajor, knocked and did not wait for my response to enter, I knew we had trouble.

She stood in the doorway, with a slightly apologetic look on her face. She held a padd in her left hand.

"What is it, Major?" I asked, my hand wrapped around my steaming—and so far untouched—glass of *raktajino*.

"I am sorry to interrupt you, Captain," she said. "But I think you need to look at this."

I should say here that Kira is one of the best officers I have on *Deep Space Nine*. She breaks protocol only when necessity calls for it. An interruption from Kira is never frivolous, and always deserves my attention.

I took the padd.

Kira nodded once, then turned and left my office, the door hissing shut behind her. Through that door, I could see my morning staff at their usual positions, and I found comfort in that. Kira spoke briefly to Jadzia Dax, a joined Trill who sat at the science station, before going to the replicator to get her own morning glass of *raktajino*.

Before I turned my attention to the padd, I took what would be my only sip of *raktajino* that day. Then I read the report the major had prepared for me.

It seems that a few moments before my arrival, the station picked up a distress call. Sent in an ancient Earth code that had not been used since the early days of human interstellar travel.

But perhaps the most intriguing feature of the distress call was that it originated in an empty area of space near the Klingon border. The area did not have a planetary system, or large space debris, and our equipment could not pick up any sign of a ship or space station for light-years around.

A distress call was coming out of nothing.

"Your equipment. Bah!" Sotugh said. His outburst startled Sisko and others around the table. "I do not think the fault was with your equipment. Your people do not know how to run a proper scan."

Sisko slid his chair back slightly. "Your people had trouble as well."

"Let him tell the story," said a humanoid woman who had been sitting at the end of the bar. She stood. She was tall and slender, with catlike features and peach fur. She kicked a chair away from the table with a dark boot, and then twisted it, so that it faced the bar. She sat on it backward, placing her arms on top of the seat, and resting her chin on her arms. "I think it's fascinating."

"You would," Sotugh snapped.

"Leave your conflicts outside," Cap said. Then he nodded to Sisko. "Please continue, Captain."

Sisko nodded in return. "The report documented the anomalies I mentioned a moment ago," he said, with a glance at Sotugh, "but I felt they were strange enough to warrant another look. . . ."

* * *

I left my office and entered Ops.

The day crew is my most experienced and efficient. My chief engineer, Miles O'Brien, had once served on the *Starship Enterprise,* and falls into that legendary category of Starfleet engineers, the kind who can make a starship out of spitballs and twine. Lieutenant Commander Worf, a Klingon . . .

Sisko looked pointedly at Sotugh as he said that. Sotugh scowled into his blood wine and said nothing.

. . . who had also served on the *Enterprise*-D under the captaincy of Jean-Luc Picard. Worf has the finest sense of honor of any Klingon I have ever met. He also values perfection and brings a level of detail to his work that I find rare even in the ranks of Starfleet.

Jadzia Dax has been my friend through two different incarnations, and I find her wisdom and intelligence an essential part of our crew. I discovered later that she was the one, not Major Kira, who discovered the distress signal. But Dax has known me a long time, and she prefers to let someone else interrupt my morning routine. It goes back to the days when Dax was joined to Curzon, a rather surly old man who influenced me more than I care to say. But that is another story, for another time.

"Major," I said as I walked down the steps to the main section of Ops. "Are you still reading the signal?"

Kira balanced her glass of *raktajino* on her knee as she glanced at her console. "Yes," she said.

"There is still nothing in that section of space," Dax said. "I have run every scan I can think of."

"As well as some she shouldn't have," Chief O'Brien said.

Dax smiled at him. "It didn't put any strain on the equipment."

"This time," he said testily.

This sort of interaction was common among my morning crew, and it rose out of their sense of perfection.

"Notify Starfleet," I said. "I would like to investigate this further, but its proximity to the Klingon border could create problems that the Federation does not need."

"Captain," Kira said, before she carried out my order. "This might be a trap."

Out of the corner of my eye I could see Dax shaking her head as she stared at her board.

"It may be a trap," Worf said from his security station, "but it is not a Klingon trap."

"Worf knows his people," Sotugh said.

Sisko took the momentary break to sip from his Jibetian ale. He wasn't used to talking this much; his mouth was getting dry already.

"So then what happened?" asked a green-skinned woman in a blazing pink uniform. Sisko wondered how, with such colors, he had missed her when he first scanned the bar.

"We notified Starfleet," Sisko said, "and they approved of the mission. I ordered the crew, along with our doctor, and several others, to be on our starship, the *Defiant,* within the hour. I left the station in Major Kira's capable hands."

"Very interesting," the catlike woman said. Perhaps it was better to describe her response as a purr. She leveled her bright green gaze on Sisko and smiled at him. "So *that* is what the Federation was doing. Yet you said this happened near the Klingon border. What were the Klingons doing?"

The dozen bar patrons sitting around the large double table shifted their attention from Sisko to Sotugh, waiting for him to answer. Cap leaned against the outside of the bar near the table, smiling. Sisko got the sense that, even though the catlike woman had directed the comment at him, she clearly had meant it as a jab at Sotugh.

But her question did seem to spark a lot of interest. A human couple, who had taken seats above the table at the bar to listen to the story, leaned forward. The woman watched closely while sipping from a cup of hot tea. The man, however, had abandoned his dark, carbonated beverage on the bar. "Yes," he said, with genuine interest, "did the Klingons hear the distress call?"

Sotugh nodded. "We did. And we understood its ancient language and message. But as Sisko said, there was nothing there. A waste of valuable time to investigate."

"Yet," the catlike woman said, still looking at Sisko, "you criticize the captain here for improperly using his equipment. What of yours?"

"We did not have time to chase ghosts in space," Sotugh said. "We trusted our readings and our equipment. Nothing was there to investigate."

"You didn't think that later," Sisko said, setting down his bottle of Jibetian ale.

"Things changed later," Sotugh said. "You are not telling everything, Sisko."

"I would, if you'd give me a chance," Sisko said evenly, making sure he was smiling.

In disgust, Sotugh downed the last of his blood wine. With a wide sweeping motion that almost caught the side of the Jibetian woman beside him, he handed his cup back to Cap, who without missing a beat slid it down the bar to Arthur, who was standing behind the bar. Obviously the young-looking Arthur was functioning as the assistant bartender.

"Please go on with your story, Captain," Cap said. "It seems clear that something was sending out that distress call after all."

Sisko raised his bottle of ale in a motion of agreement. "Oh, there was a ship sending out the distress call, all right. But our instruments, and Sotugh's, were correct. There was nothing there."

Sisko smiled at the puzzled expression on Cap's face before taking another long drink and going back to his story.

CHAPTER
3

THE *DEFIANT* is the toughest starship in the Federation. It is sleek and streamlined, yet has more power than the Galaxy-class starships most people think of when they hear the word "Starfleet." The *Defiant* can run efficiently with a minimal crew. It is also the first Federation ship to be equipped with a cloaking device, a fact that we have relied on greatly in our current conflict with the Dominion.

I must be honest with you: As much as I like running the station, I love captaining the *Defiant.* When I sit on the command chair in the center of that bridge, I feel the way I always imagined I would feel when I was a boy dreaming of a career in the stars. Captaining the *Defiant,* even when we take her out on a routine maintenance spin to see if her parts are in working order, is like I imagine captaining an old seafaring vessel would have been. Sometimes I think, as the docking clamps release and the ship heads out into the blackness of space, *There be dragons here.*

I know that Dax shares my feelings, for whenever she and I stand on the bridge together, she gives me a look filled with mischief and awe. In her eyes, I see old Curzon and hear his lusty laugh as we are about to embark on yet another adventure.

There are adventures on *Deep Space Nine,* often more adventures than I would care for, but there the adventure seems to come to us.

On the *Defiant,* we head out into territories unknown, seeking the adventures ourselves.

That day, I thought of the old sailing maps and dragons as I sat on the command chair. I should have been thinking more along the line of pirates.

Dax had the helm. Behind me, Chief O'Brien was checking the systems. Commander Worf was checking our route, scanning as per my order, for anything that might seem like a trap. Should anything happen, he would be in charge of our weaponry. Cadet Nog, the first Ferengi to serve in Starfleet, monitored our communications.

Our station's chief medical officer, Julian Bashir, was powering up sickbay. I had a hunch—not an entirely pleasant one—that we would need his services before the adventure ended. I have found, in my years at *Deep Space Nine,* that leadership is one-third knowledge, one-third common sense, and one-third a deep-in-your-heart, unprovable moment of absolute certainty, based solely on pure gut instinct. The best leaders learn how to separate that instinct from wishful thinking. It is, I think, the hardest thing of all to do, even harder than preparing a beloved crew for war.

It was Cadet Nog who set the tone for the early part of this mission. I saw many of you frown when you heard me mention that a Ferengi had gone to Starfleet Academy, but he had done so at my recommendation. The very features that make Ferengi the true capitalists of the Alpha Quadrant are the features that will make Nog into one of Starfleet's best officers one day. Not their unmistakable avarice, but their attention to detail, their willingness to learn anything if it will benefit them, and their complete desire to be the best at anything they do.

Nog has never forgotten that it was my recommendation that opened the doors to Starfleet Academy, and he has been trying, in the most earnest manner I have ever seen, to repay me ever since.

For my part, I test him at every opportunity I get. At first, I did so because I did not want this recommendation to haunt me in future years, but later, the tests became my way of setting the bar as high as possible for the young cadet. I see in him officer material if he can shed a few of his Ferengi habits.

We had barely cleared the station when Nog said, "The distress signal continues, Captain." His voice was steady, considering he was only a cadet at the time, and it was his first time on the *Defiant*.

From my position, I could not see the cadet without turning my head. But I had a clear view of the side of Dax's face. She was grinning at Nog's obvious excitement. Like me, she felt responsible for the boy, and liked to encourage him. So she said, "There's still no sign of a ship, Benjamin. Or even debris."

"I do not like this," Worf said. "I recommend we go into the area with shields up."

"Noted," I said.

Worf had a point. With tensions running as high as they were at that time in the Alpha Quadrant, we could have been heading into something quite unpleasant. We had also had enough experiences this deep in space to show us that nothing was impossible.

Now, please understand another reason for my desire to explore this strange signal. I am rather fond of stories of lost ships. We had found one once, earlier in my tenure at *Deep Space Nine,* and I had been harboring a secret hope that we were about to find another.

"Old man," I said to Dax. "Are there any records of lost ships in this area from the time of that signal?"

Dax shook her head. "The signal dates from the early days of Earth's expansion out to the stars. They didn't keep the kinds of records we keep now. In those days more ships vanished than reported back."

I knew that, and I knew that the list of possible candidates would be endless. In addition to ships of exploration, many of those early Earth ships were colony ships, leaving Earth never intending to return. Only a few of them had found homes.

The distress signal continued as we approached its coordinates. As we reached the right area I asked Chief O'Brien if he had found the signal's source.

24

"No, sir," O'Brien said, not taking his eyes off his panel. He had calibrated one of the ship's sensors to search for any signs of a technology that might be hiding a ship or any unusual space anomalies. "In fact, I'm not finding anything at all. Frankly, sir, I don't like this."

Now, I have been on countless missions with the chief, and on many of them, he did not locate the source of the problem we were investigating on his first pass. His comment surprised and intrigued me.

"What exactly don't you like, Chief?" I asked.

He shook his head while continuing to stare at his panel. "Not only is there nothing in the area of that signal, but the entire area of space for almost a light-year in diameter is clear of all debris. Even the dust molecule content is way, way down."

"That cannot be," Worf said.

Now I understood what he was talking about. Even though space seems empty, it never is. There is always some form of matter in forms of asteroids or small dust clouds too thin for the naked eye to see.

"What would wipe an entire area of space clean?" Dax asked.

"I do not see how such a thing is even remotely possible," Worf said.

"I find it curious," I said, "that we would be getting a distress call from an area of space so empty that a dustball would seem conspicuous." I leaned forward. The display on the screen before me showed only darkness.

No one had a response for that, so I said, "Okay,

old man, take us in slow and easy. Mr. Worf, go to alert status. Screens up."

"Aye, Captain."

The sound of the relief in Worf's voice made me smile slightly. Dax also smiled in fond amusement without taking her attention from her controls. Recently Dax and Worf married, but at the time of this mission, their relationship had not yet begun. I saw the relationship reflected in tiny gestures like Dax's. It did not interfere with their duties and seemed to make them even more efficient officers.

The chief's mention of discomfort seemed to travel through the crew. I was cautious, but not uncomfortable. I was fascinated by the puzzle, and ready to discover the secrets behind it.

I would discover those secrets sooner than I expected.

"We're almost on top of the signal," Dax said.

"We are less than one thousand meters away," Worf said.

"Chief?" I asked, without turning from the empty space showing on the viewscreen in front of me.

"I'm still not reading anything," he said.

"Have you checked the systems?"

"They're fine, sir. The problem isn't us." He turned and pointed at the blackness on the screen. "It's out there."

"That signal *has* to be coming from somewhere, people," I said, putting an edge in my voice. I wanted an answer before we got into a situation we could not predict. "It could be a cloaked ship, a time anomaly, anything. And I want to know what."

"We are five hundred meters away, Captain," Dax said, reverting from the familiar to my title, as she usually did in military situations.

"Take us to two hundred meters and hold that position," I said.

It took only a moment for Dax to report, "All stop. We are two hundred meters from the point of the distress call."

I still saw only emptiness on the viewscreen. "Magnify," I said.

"We're already at full magnification, sir," O'Brien said. "At this range, we would be able to see the pattern in the metal on the side of any ship."

I leaned forward, intrigued and mystified. There was a distress call coming from a point so close I could almost reach out and touch it, and yet nothing was there. Not even space dust.

"The message continues to repeat," O'Brien said, "coming from a point one hundred meters directly in front of us. Nothing is there that any of my instruments can see."

"How can that be?" I asked. I was ready for some answers. I was tired of my crew telling me that they found nothing. Something had to be sending that distress call, even if it was a carrier wave bouncing off something in space.

"It's impossible," the chief said, "but that's what's happening."

"Chief, *something* is causing that signal."

"No, sir," the chief said, sounding more rattled than usual. "Nothing is. I've explored every possibility, and I can't find anything."

"Then, you haven't explored every possibility," I said. "Cadet, what, exactly, is the source of that signal?"

"Ah, sir, I'm not reading a source." Nog sounded almost frightened of me. Which was good. I wanted to scare a bit of efficiency into my normally brilliant crew.

"There must be a source, Cadet."

"Benjamin," Dax said softly, almost protectively, "they're right. There is no source. Only coordinates."

"So," I said, "you're telling me that if we moved the *Defiant* directly over that point, the message would come from right here on the bridge?"

The chief stood near full attention. He knew I wasn't happy.

Dax sighed.

Worf continued to run scans.

I turned slightly, and saw the cadet look from one senior officer to another, hoping they knew the answer that he did not. In all my years of service with this crew, I had never seen them so completely baffled.

"I would not recommend such an action, sir," Worf said, after a short moment.

"Actually, Commander," I said, turning to look at Mr. Worf, forcing myself not to smile, "I wasn't considering it. I was merely asking."

"In that case, sir," Worf said, "it would seem that your analysis is correct."

I didn't like that answer at all, but no one else contradicted him. "Do you have a better idea on how to discover what's out there?" I asked.

Worf looked me right in the eye, straightened his back slightly, and said, "I do not, sir."

"Sir!" Nog shouted.

I spun around to face the now far-from-empty viewscreen.

Where a moment before had been nothing but very empty vacuum was now a long slit, as if the fabric of space had just been ripped open. The edges of the split were shimmering as it expanded and opened, sending a faint cloud of mist into the void.

"What is that?" I asked.

"It's as if space just ruptured," Dax said sharply. "We're too close."

"Get us out of here, old man," I said.

"I can't," she said. "Too late."

The tear in space moved over and around us, like a giant mouth of a fish swallowing us whole.

The ship remained completely silent. No rumble, no movement.

Nothing.

Everything remained normal as the cloud passed over us and disappeared, all in just a fraction of a second.

Again the screen in front of me only showed space, but where there had been nothing but emptiness for light-years, there were now suns and planetary systems.

Impossible suns and planetary systems.

Yet they were there. And we were just outside one of the systems.

But they were not the most startling change. That appeared directly in front of us. An alien craft now dominated our viewscreen.

Shiny black, it was shaped like two swept-back wings that met in the middle, with no body in between. It seemed to hover in space instead of float, bringing back memories of hawks diving at mice and eagles soaring. In all my years of seeing alien craft, I had never seen such a beautiful, and deadly-looking, craft.

It was my first sight of a ship of the Mist.

The fire to Sisko's back popped slightly, but otherwise there were no sounds in the entire bar. Everyone was listening to his story. He paused and took a long drink of ale, signaling that others should do the same. Sisko glanced around at his listeners. They did, but reluctantly, as if unwilling to break the story's spell.

Even Sotugh had been interested, although Sisko would not have known that if he had not spent a lot of time observing Worf. Klingons had a unique ability to look distracted when they were concentrating hard.

The Jibetian ale soothed the dryness in Sisko's throat. He took a second sip before satisfying a question of his own.

"So, Sotugh," Sisko asked. "Is this the point you got interested in the distress call?"

Sotugh laughed. "Of course, Captain," he said, leaning forward over his mug of blood wine. "We were monitoring your little rescue mission from the moment you left your station. When your ship disappeared, your mission became more than one of curiosity. Suddenly it became a threat to the Empire."

Sisko nodded, hoping Sotugh would continue.

Sotugh sat back, obviously—and surprisingly—not going to say another word.

Sisko studied him over the bottle of Jibetian ale. Sotugh was not going to make the telling of this story easy in any fashion.

"Your ship *disappeared?*" the catlike woman asked, glancing first at Sisko, then back at Sotugh.

"So, Captain," Cap said. "Don't hold us in suspense. What happened next?"

Sisko smiled, settled into a more comfortable position, and told them.

CHAPTER
4

I STOOD. I did not like this new ship, this position, or these new impossible stars and systems.

"Dax," I said, "where are we?"

"According to my sensors, we haven't moved, Captain."

"We are at the same coordinates," Worf said, confirming what Dax had said.

"The distress call is gone," Nog said.

Something was very, very wrong. We had been lured here. My feeling had been right. Here there were dragons; there was one before us, and I was not pleased.

I returned to my chair. "I want to know who that ship belongs to and what it wants with us," I said. I sat forward and studied it.

The ship was beautiful in a way that even now I cannot describe. Its design looked aerodynamic, as if the ship would function well in atmosphere, under water, or in space. Upon closer observation, the two wings, which had seemed attached to each other a moment before, had a small bulge between them, as unnoticeable as the body of a monarch butterfly or a Carnuiin round beetle. Both wings tapered back to fine points. No ports or weapons marred the perfect gleaming black surfaces.

"I'm not finding this ship anywhere in our database," Dax said. "The computer can't match it, and I've never seen anything like it."

That was quite a statement. In her many lives, Dax had seen a multitude of ships.

"I believe their shields are up," Worf said. "These readings are clear, but I do not trust them. They do not seem to be powering their weapons, but that does not mean they are not doing so."

"Let me know the moment the situation changes, Mr. Worf."

"Aye, sir."

I frowned at the ship. I blamed it for our transfer to this new place, even though I did not yet know exactly what, or where, this new place was. At that point, I was wondering how we had moved from one area of space to another without our instruments reflecting it.

"Captain," Chief O'Brien said. "That empty area of space I mentioned. It's no longer empty."

"I noticed, Chief."

"I mean, everything's back. The space dust. The debris. Everything that should be in an area of space."

"And five star systems," Dax added. "All inhabited."

"Most likely by the people who built that ship in front of us," I said.

"Those systems are stable," O'Brien said. "They weren't just moved there. It's as if they've *always* been right there. But they are on no modern star charts, and they weren't there a minute ago."

I was becoming more and more convinced that space hadn't changed, but that we had. "I want a double check of our equipment. I want to know if our coordinates have changed."

"My readings show they haven't," Dax said.

"I don't care about your readings," I said. "It seems to me that our systems might have been affected by that strange rupture we experienced. I want to know if we have found a wormhole, perhaps, or something else, something that moved us from one area of space to another."

"Nothing in our systems show that, Captain," Worf said. "I have already performed the necessary checks. If we have shifted positions, then our readings do not and will not show it."

"What about time?" I asked. If we remained in the same area of space, perhaps we had moved either forward or backward in time. That, too, had happened before, and it was unsettling to say the least. It would explain, however, why the distress signal had disappeared, and why the interplanetary systems had appeared.

"No, sir," Worf said. "We seem to be in the same place in time as we were when everything changed."

"I've scanned for chroniton particles, sir," O'Brien said. "They were the first things I scanned for, and I haven't found anything."

"Cadet, has that ship made any attempt to contact us?" I asked.

"Not yet, sir."

I glanced at him over my shoulder. "Do you expect them to?"

"If a ship mysteriously appeared in my path, sir, I would hail them. Sir."

"As would I," I said. "Dax, scan the surrounding area. See what else has changed."

While she worked, I stared at the ship facing us, and the impossible star systems behind it. Moving or hiding inhabited star systems just wasn't something that was done. At least not by any science known to the Alpha Quadrant. The bridge was silent except for the beep of consoles as my crew tried to determine exactly what had happened to us.

"Captain," Dax said, her fingers flying over the board in front of her. *"Deep Space Nine* is still in place and it seems to be functioning normally. We are still on the border of the Klingon Empire, and nothing about those systems seems different either."

Of all of the news I had just received, that was the part I did not like. If the star system had simply appeared, why hadn't *Deep Space Nine* disappeared?

I turned to the chief. "Are there differences between the readings we're taking of *Deep Space Nine,* and the readings we're getting of these new star systems?"

35

"Sir?" O'Brien asked, in that vaguely puzzled tone that he always used when he didn't understand one of my orders.

"I am thinking that perhaps the ship and the systems—"

"Were planted into our data systems," Dax said. "Of course." She bent over her console. So did the chief and Worf.

They all looked at me at the same time, and I knew before anyone spoke what their responses would be.

"I'm sorry, sir," O'Brien started. "But—"

"Captain," Worf said. "Three Klingon ships have just crossed the border. They are heading for our position."

Of course. The shift had attracted their attention. Not the first time I welcomed the arrival of the Klingons.

"That is," Sotugh said, "because you could not handle what you saw."

Every patron froze. The woman who was part of the middle-aged human couple at the bar said, a thread of irritation clear in her voice, "It seems to me that the captain was doing just fine."

"Fine," Sotugh said. "If he had been doing fine, he would not have needed help."

"Don't throw stones, Sotugh," Sisko said softly. "Your part in this tale is still ahead of us."

Sotugh stood abruptly and headed to the bar. He slammed his mug of blood wine on the wood, and the sound echoed. The strange alien at the piano brushed against the keys, seemingly accidentally, but the instrument mirrored the sound Sotugh had just made.

Sotugh ignored it. "More blood wine," he said. "And this time, make sure it is true blood wine."

"Our drinks are authentic," Cap said evenly. During Sisko's tale, he had moved from the front of the bar to the back. "Perhaps you would like some blood wine that dates from a different time period? The days of Kahless, perhaps?"

"Do not toy with me, bartender," Sotugh said. "Sisko's lies have put me in a disagreeable mood."

"How strange for a Klingon," the catlike woman said.

"I want to hear the rest," said a small, bristly alien with a large snout. He was standing on a chair toward the back, his chin barely crossing its top.

Sisko nodded to him. "As I said," Sisko continued, "three Klingon ships had just crossed the border. . . ."

"Dax," I said, "when will the Klingons arrive?"

"In sixteen minutes," Dax said.

I hoped we would have some answers by then.

"Bah!" Sotugh said from the bar.

"Sotugh," the catlike woman cautioned. "Let the man talk."

"Everything changed when that cloud surrounded us," I said. "Let's analyze that."

"I have been," O'Brien said. "I kept thinking that it was the cause of the change, but I can't see what it's

37

done. It went over us, and everything changed, but I don't know if that's because it went over us, or if it appeared just as the ship did."

"They did not even scan us," Worf said.

"The ship or the cloudlike thing?" I asked.

"Neither," Worf said.

I stared at the ship floating in the center of the viewscreen, silently watching us. There didn't seem to be much choice. Since we had no idea what happened, and since it didn't look like we were going to figure it out soon, we had to gather more information.

"Hail the ship," I said.

"Aye, sir," Nog said. Then he bounced in his chair, unable to contain his excitement. "They're answering us, sir."

"Put them on the screen, Cadet."

I stood just as the screen flickered and changed. To my great surprise, the image of another human being faced me. Beside and slightly behind him was a thin, tall, almost wisplike humanoid of a species I had never seen before. The alien had a thin face with large, pupilless eyes and an even larger partially open mouth.

The human wore an unfamiliar gold uniform topped by a gold yachting cap. His hair and skin were dark, his eyes a vibrant blue. He had broad shoulders, a large smile, and was clearly in command. The alien also wore a form of the gold uniform, only without the yachting cap around his bald head. On the alien the uniform looked like a robe.

"Captain Sisko," the human said. "It's a pleasure meeting you. I'm Captain Victor and this is Councillor Näna of the High Council."

His use of my name made me instantly wary, but I did not show it. Instead, I said, "Was it your distress call that we answered?"

Captain Victor smiled and nodded. "Actually, it was a far distant ancestor's of mine. My family's name was Tucker. We left Earth hundreds of years ago in a ship called the *Dorren*. I just borrowed that distant relative's distress call to attract you."

"Obviously, it worked," I said, this time letting more of my displeasure show. "But you are clearly not in distress. Why didn't you contact us directly instead of using an ancient distress call to set a trap?"

"How can you judge on such a brief meeting, Captain, whether or not we are in distress?" he asked, but the question sounded lighthearted.

"We do not take distress calls lightly," I said.

"We know. That's why we used one to contact you."

"What do you want with us?" I asked.

Captain Victor laughed. "The answers to some of those questions will take a long time to explain. However, we used the ancient distress call to achieve the exact result we got. You came and the Klingons didn't."

"I'm afraid they're on their way now."

Captain Victor waved a hand as if brushing away a fly. "They can send as many ships as they want. It will make no difference to us."

"Captain!" Cadet Nog broke in. "I'm getting—"

"Not now, Cadet," I said without taking my gaze away from the screen.

"Captain, sir!" Nog said. "This is important."

I hoped Nog was right. He was still very new to Starfleet protocol. "Excuse me," I said to Captain Victor. Then I turned to Nog. "This had better be good, Cadet."

"Sir," Nog said, swallowing hard, "the station is hailing us on all emergency frequencies. And they have dispatched ships to search for us."

"To search for us?" I asked.

Again Cadet Nog swallowed hard, then looked up at me. "They seem to think we've vanished."

"You have," Captain Victor said, smiling. "At least as far as your station is concerned."

Behind him, Councillor Nāna only nodded, his mouth opening and closing slowly.

"Your disappearance surprised us all," Sotugh said, returning to his chair, the blood wine sloshing out of his mug.

For the first time, Sotugh's interruption didn't seem to bother the other patrons. Only the catlike woman glared at him.

"How did the *Defiant*'s sudden vanishing act seem to other ships?" Cap asked Sotugh.

"There was no energy surge, no sudden movement," Sotugh said, shaking his head in disgust at the memory. "The ship simply vanished from our screens at the exact same moment the ancient distress call stopped. Ships do not vanish in open space."

"Unless they're cloaked," the bristly alien said.

"We know how to read the energy signature of a cloaked ship," Sotugh said with less annoyance than Sisko would have expected at such a comment.

"So you were coming to investigate," the middle-aged man at the bar said.

"Of course," Sotugh said, his words becoming almost a snarl. "We assumed the Federation was testing a new weapon to be turned against the Empire."

"If we were," Sisko said, "we wouldn't have done so that near the Klingon border."

"Your people can be sneaky, Sisko. It might have been a way of warning us."

"Logical," Cap said, nodding his head.

"And very Klingon," Sisko said.

"You would have done the same," Sotugh said.

Smiling, Sisko raised his ale bottle to Sotugh. "I would have."

Yellowish light flooded the entryway to the bar.

Sisko and a few of the others at the large table turned slightly to look. The door had opened, but then closed before he could see who had come inside.

"Arthur," Cap said. "Make sure everyone who needs a drink gets one. I'll greet our new guest."

Sisko held up his now almost empty bottle of ale for Arthur to see, then watched as Cap moved down the bar just as a Trill came around the corner from the front entry, his eyes blinking as he fought to adjust to the dim light. He was young, dressed in a thick jacket of unfamiliar design, and looked cold. Sisko found that odd, since the day outside was one of the hottest Sisko could remember in this area of Bajor.

The Trill had short hair, his neck markings clearly visible. He smiled at the group, but the smile was tired.

Sisko frowned at him. He had seen the Trill before; he was sure of it. But not that sure. Sisko never forgot a face, and he knew—just as clearly as he knew that he'd seen the Trill—that he hadn't seen the Trill look quite like this.

Besides that, what was a Trill doing on Bajor, in a bar? Sisko made a mental note to ask the Trill if he got the chance.

"Welcome, Captain," Cap said to the Trill. "We have a warm fire and anything you care to drink."

Sisko watched as the Trill nodded, seemingly relieved to take off his coat and warm up. The silence in the bar was palpable and, of course, the Trill noticed.

"I'm sorry," he said. "I didn't mean to interrupt."

"Yes," Sotugh said. "Continue your story. There is much drinking to do."

"And, it seems," the catlike woman said, "much story left to tell."

"There is, at that," Sisko said. He took the new ale from Arthur, and then, with one more glance at the new arrival, went back to his story of the Mist.

42

CHAPTER
5

I WAS TRYING to comprehend all of the information I had just received. The station had sent out calls on all emergency frequencies searching for us; it had also sent ships. The Klingons were coming, in three ships as well. They had not answered the distress call, but they were coming now.

And this man on the screen in front of me, this Captain Victor, was telling me that we had vanished, that he and his friend, Councillor Näna, had lured us with the distress call as bait, and then reeled us in with the cloud of mist once we arrived.

I did not like being the fish.

I made a small motion to Cadet Nog, indicating that I wanted the sound momentarily severed between us and Captain Victor. I turned, as if I were surveying my crew, and said softly, in case Nog had misunderstood the order, "I want you all to check and see if there is anything different about our ship,

43

whether they have cloaked us, or if there is something different on a molecular level. Do so quickly and with no communication."

Then I signaled Nog to continue the sound as if it had not been cut off. I finished my scan of the bridge and turned back to the screen.

"Satisfied, Captain?" Victor said to me. "Do you see now that the others believe you are gone?"

"What I see," I said calmly, even though I was not feeling calm, "is that somehow our signals and signatures are not reaching the others. I am not prepared to say that we have vanished."

Then I made a show of turning to Nog. "Answer the station, Cadet. Give them our location, and tell them that, for the moment, we are all right."

"Aye, sir," Nog said, looking at me rather strangely. It was Starfleet protocol to answer any emergency hail. I could tell from his expression that he had already done so and had received no response. I did not care. I wanted him to do so again, while Victor and Näna watched, so that we could observe any manipulation they might be causing. Perhaps our equipment would be able to locate what was causing the change in instruments.

For that was all I believed it to be, at the time. My mind did not accept that entire planetary systems could be invisible. I believed we were in the grip of a massive, and highly advanced, cloaking system. I knew that some planets had their own cloaking system, and we had, of course, the technology to cloak ships. It was a small stretch to believe that we could cloak entire areas of space as well.

A small stretch was all that I was willing to take.

"You know they can't hear you," Captain Victor said.

I felt my eyes narrow and my entire face become rigid. Whenever I got that look, my wife used to say, entire galaxies would crumble.

Captain Victor did not flinch. I decided to say nothing to him at the moment. Nothing would be more productive than the things I was thinking.

I turned to Nog, partly to prevent myself from saying anything to Victor. "Is there any response, Cadet?"

"No, sir," Nog said.

"Commander Worf, what about the Klingons?" I asked.

If I looked angry, Worf looked thunderous. "We are sending, sir, but there is no response. They, too, are acting as if we have disappeared."

"You have," Captain Victor said, his smile reaching his blue eyes almost as laughter.

I wanted to cut off all communication with that man. But I did not. I continued to ignore him, until I could put the situation back under my control.

"Check everything," I ordered my staff. "And keep trying to hail the station and the Klingons."

Then I turned back to face the screen. "All right, Captain," I said, with a slight sarcastic emphasis on the word *Captain*. "You seem to have all the answers. Share them."

"Gladly, Captain," Victor said. He glanced at his companion. Councillor Năna had still said nothing. His round mouth opened and closed occasionally, as if the movement were involuntary.

"A few moments ago," Victor said, "you couldn't see our ship or our homeworlds, could you?"

"No," I said. I knew what he was going to say, and I knew it would not be the answer I wanted. I wanted whys, not whats.

"Now," he said, "you and your fine ship have simply moved into our reality."

"The shimmering opening," O'Brien murmured.

Victor heard him. "It is a sort of doorway."

"It is not that simple," I said, this time letting the anger I felt punctuate each word. It was as if I put a space between each one.

"No, it's not," Victor said. "I would gladly explain everything to you, including our motives. But I think it might be better if you first moved your ship out of your current position."

"You want us out of your doorway," I said, not willing to move. I wanted to get out of there, and to do so now. I did not like how any of this was going.

Captain Victor laughed. "Of course not. That opening can be made anywhere with the right equipment. I'm just trying to save you some massive disorientation when the Klingon ships arrive."

At that moment, I did not understand what he meant. I would shortly.

"We've handled Klingons before," I said. "We will stay right here."

"Be my guest," Captain Victor said, shrugging as if he really didn't much care. "We'll move a short distance away and stand by. We've found it's just easier."

"Easier than what?" I asked.

"You'll see," Victor said, and then winked off the screen. In his place, his beautiful spaceship appeared, with the stars beyond it. The ship was moving slightly.

I sighed. "Once," I said, "just once, I would like to encounter a strange group who did not enjoy being mysterious."

No one laughed. No one was supposed to.

I sat down in my command chair, and surveyed the bridge. My crew was working as efficiently as always, but beneath that efficiency was a tension that I had seldom felt before.

"What are our new friends doing, Mr. Worf?" I asked.

"They appear to be changing position," he said.

"Just like Captain Victor said they would," Dax said.

I nodded.

"Captain," Worf said, "the Klingon ships are still heading this way."

"Have they responded to our hails yet?" I asked.

"No, sir, but they are heading directly for us."

"Is this some type of battlefield behavior that I'm not familiar with, Mr. Worf?"

"No, sir."

I frowned. "Let me know when they get here."

"Aye, sir," Worf said.

"Still no response from *Deep Space Nine,* sir," Nog said, anticipating my next question.

"The station is acting exactly by the book," Dax said, "following procedures that indicate there's an emergency on a ship. To the station we've gone missing."

I nodded as on the screen the alien ship turned like a bird on a gentle wind and moved off at slow impulse.

"Keep a very close eye on them, Mr. Worf," I said.

"I have been, Captain," Worf said. Then he bent his head slightly. "Captain, the Klingon ships will arrive in less than a minute. They are heading directly for our position."

"Hail them, Cadet. On all channels. Priority one."

"Yes, sir," Nog said.

I drummed my fingers on the arm of my chair. Victor wanted us to move out of the way of the Klingons. He knew that something was going to happen. Perhaps the Klingons couldn't see us. But they would be able to read our energy signature. Klingons knew how to search for cloaked ships.

"I'm getting no response, sir," Nog said.

"Captain," Worf said, "the Klingon ships are approaching uncloaked and fast. They have shields up, but have no weapons powered."

"Acting as if they don't see us," Dax said to herself.

"Hold this position. These are the last coordinates they had for us. They will search for us here," I said.

"And continue hailing both the station and the approaching Klingon ships."

"Yes, sir," Nog said.

"Klingon ships dropping to impulse, slowing," Dax said.

That was what I had wanted to hear. I had expected it, but I was relieved nonetheless. The alien ship had settled into a position some distance from its original spot, but it was still close to us.

"Cadet, have you reached the Klingon ships?" I asked.

"No, sir. There's still no response." Nog's voice went up as it usually did when he panicked. But he was working hard, no matter how out of control he sounded.

"The lead Klingon ship is a Vor'Cha-class battle cruiser, the *Daqchov,*" Worf said. "HoD Sotugh in command. He is not usually like this. He is quite responsive—"

"Too fast!" Dax said. "Two thousand meters and closing too fast. They don't see us."

I had not expected this. I had thought they would come near these coordinates, not fly through them. "Get us out of their way!"

My order came too late.

As the *Defiant* moved, the *Daqchov* suddenly was on top of us, and then without the slightest hint of impact, we were inside the *Daqchov.*

Not just rammed through the side, but we actually passed through their hull. For a brief instant I got a glimpse of Sotugh sitting in his command chair, seemingly interested in his viewscreen, but clearly not braced for any impact.

Then a wave of nausea swept over me, as if the entire world had been turned inside out, along with the insides of my ear. I had no memory of ever being so dizzy before. The ship spun, and I had to cling to my command chair to keep my balance.

The rest of the crew was clinging too.

We were all superimposed on the inside of the *Daqchov.* It was as if the *Daqchov* had swallowed the *Defiant,* as if we all occupied the same space, like two holographic images, one on top of the other.

As we moved apart, Klingon hands went through me, Klingon equipment slid through my chair, and Klingon hull went through our bridge.

Then, as quickly as it had happened, the *Daqchov* was gone, back outside in space where it belonged.

"Damage reports?" I asked, my voice clear despite my dizziness.

"None, Captain." Dax sounded as shaky as I felt. Shaky and shocked.

My eyes had not lied to me. Part of the Klingon ship had passed right through the *Defiant* without any impact. That wasn't possible, yet my eyes and my twisted stomach told me it was.

Somehow, the *Defiant* had become a ghost ship.

And we were all the ghosts.

"Ghosts?" the catlike woman said. "But you weren't dead." She plucked on his sleeve to emphasize her point. "How could you be a ghost?"

Sisko smiled. The entire crowd in the bar was watching him. Most had empty glasses or mugs. He suspected Cap was not happy about that.

"Believe me, I wondered," Sisko said. "All that training from my Earth upbringing. All those superstitions rose in my head and were as quickly discarded. But they were there. I wondered if perhaps we had died and had not known it."

"Amazing," the woman at the bar said.

"Later," Sisko said, "Chief O'Brien said he had wondered the same thing. Worf seemed quite shocked as well. I know that the Klingons are superstitious people, but he has never spoken of that moment. Nog could not keep quiet about it when we returned to the station, and it was there I learned that the Ferengi view of the afterlife is, as we all suspected, different from ours. It has something to do with profit and latinum—and nothing to do with ghosts."

"So what had actually happened?" asked the middle-aged man at the bar.

"I'll get to that," Sisko said, "as soon as everyone has a moment to refill their drinks." He looked around the bar to see where he could get rid of some of his.

"Cap," he said as he stood. "Would it be possible to get something to snack on while I finish this?"

"This story will take forever the way he is telling it," Sotugh said. "You had better feed us."

Cap smiled.

Sisko got out of his chair. His body creaked slightly. He had been sitting awhile. Sotugh was right; it was taking him a while to tell this story. But then, it had taken time to happen. His audience seemed interested, and as long as he had them, he could tell the story the way he wanted to.

He scanned the bar for the rest room.

Cap noticed what he was doing and nodded toward the back of the bar.

Sisko walked past the serving station, past some stairs, and across from a storage room he found the bathroom. He wasn't the only one who needed to use it; it seemed his entire audience stood after he did, using his break as an excuse for one of their own.

When he returned, the drinks were replenished, and bowls of bright green Betazoid fruitnuts graced each table. Sotugh had clearly complained about the choice. Before him, Cap had placed some *bregit* lung, a Klingon dish I hadn't thought possible to get in a bar like this on Bajor.

Another bottle of Jibetian ale sat in front of Sisko's place. He had had more to drink since he'd come in here than he'd had in months, but he wasn't feeling any effects yet. He wondered if it would hit him all at once.

He decided that he didn't care. Bashir had ordered him to relax and that was what he was doing. If they needed him, they knew where to find him.

"Where was I?" he asked as he sat down.

"Ghosts," several people said at once.

He smiled again. "Ah, yes," he said, and continued.

* * *

Our ships had separated, but my crew and I were still feeling the effects of the strange collision. We were all dizzy. Chief O'Brien was a pale shade of green. Cadet Nog had his hands on his lobes, as if he were trying to balance himself by holding his ears in a level position. At that moment, if that had worked for humans, I would have done the same thing.

Dizziness for a human is bad. I imagine that for a Ferengi it is intolerable.

Worf was clutching both sides of his console, but staring straight ahead.

Dax had her head bent, her eyes closed.

We all seemed to breathe in at the same time, to exhale together, as we tried to readjust our systems. Mine came under control quickly. Cadet Nog did not seem so lucky.

I was about to say something when the door to the turbolift opened, and our ship's doctor, Julian Bashir, staggered onto the bridge. He looked almost as green as the chief.

"What in heaven's name was that?" he asked. He put a hand out, used one of the consoles to keep his balance, and then steadied himself. "One moment I was getting sickbay ready, the next thing I know, sickbay has been invaded by a Klingon ship, and then suddenly, the thing is gone. *What happened?*"

"I'll tell you as soon as we know, Doctor," I said. "Dax, where are the Klingons now?"

"Setting up positions two thousand meters from our present location."

53

"Keep an eye on them. I don't want a repeat of that."

"Neither do I," Dax said.

Nog was leaning against his console to keep his head from moving. "Captain," he said, his voice a shadow of its former self, "Captain Victor is hailing us."

"Put him on screen," I said.

This time, the screen filled with Victor's face. I could not see the rest of his bridge or Councillor Näna. Victor pretended to show concern, but his blue eyes were twinkling. I didn't like or trust this man.

"Mistrusting him seems appropriate to me," Sotugh muttered into his blood wine. "You should have shot him on sight."

Sisko grinned at Sotugh. "That seemed appropriate to me too. But Starfleet wouldn't have approved."

"Starfleet does not approve of many appropriate things," Sotugh said.

"What did Victor say?" Cap asked.

"Are you and your crew recovering?" Victor asked. "The experience is not harmful, but not pleasant, either."

"We seemed to have survived whatever just happened with only a few lingering side effects," I said.

Now Captain Victor actually let himself chuckle. "The side effects will pass. But now do you understand why we moved out of the way of the Klingon ships?"

I did not answer his question. "I think it's time for that explanation," I said.

Captain Victor's smile grew. "Since I assume you would still like to remain in this area, would you like to join me on my bridge, or may I join you?"

I wasn't about to go to their bridge. "You are welcome to come on board here," I said.

Victor nodded, as if he expected me to say that.

"Mr. Worf," I said, "lower the shields."

The screen went blank. Then, before Worf could voice the objection I was sure he was going to voice, Captain Victor shimmered into form, facing me.

He had beamed through our shields, an event I didn't like in the slightest.

I stood slowly to make sure that my balance had returned. It hadn't completely. The cabin spun, as if the ship were out of control. Only I knew all the spinning was going on inside my own head. "Welcome, Captain," I managed to say.

"Please sit," Victor said, smiling. "I know how you must feel after passing through the Klingon ship."

I did not sit down. It was my ship, and I would be the one who gave the commands. Although I did wish that I had not stood up.

Slowly, the spinning eased.

"You promised answers," I said.

He nodded and walked to the main screen. I noted that all the members of my crew, from the doctor to Dax, watched him closely. If Victor tried anything, I doubted anyone on my crew would hesitate. He would find himself on the floor, stunned by a phaser, in a matter of seconds.

Apparently my crew disliked being dizzy as much as I did. And they seemed to distrust this Captain Victor as much as I did.

He stopped and faced the main screen in such a manner that he could partially face me and partially face the screen.

"I'll make this as quick as I can," he said. "There isn't much time."

I waited.

"The five systems you see in front of you," he said, pointing at the screen, "are the homeworlds of the Mist."

"The Mist?" I asked.

This time it was Dax who nodded. She was still staring at Captain Victor. "Of course," she said. "That's what happened to them."

She spoke as if everything had become clear to her.

It was not yet clear to me. Not in the slightest.

CHAPTER 6

THE DIZZINESS HAD VANISHED, leaving only a slight ringing in my ears. I barely noticed the change. I was watching Captain Victor. He was watching me, apparently to gauge my reaction.

"Dax," I said. "You know of this?"

"I know of the Mist," she said. "But I'd rather hear what Captain Victor has to say."

"As would I," Worf said. Somehow his curt, clipped tone made those three words sound like a threat. Victor caught the implication too.

"I only know the Mist as a legend," I said. "Like the ancient Greek gods from Earth, or the bottle creatures from the lost worlds of Ythi Four."

"Yeah," O'Brien said. "I rather feel like an Englishman in Ireland, being told the little people are real."

"The Mist are real enough," Victor said.

"So how do real beings become legend and not get discovered?" I asked.

Victor glanced at the screen, a half-smile playing on his face. Then, with a dramatic sweep of his arm, he pointed toward the five star systems behind the Mist ship. "At one time," he said, "those five systems were in normal space. This was over a thousand years before Cochrane invented the first human warp drive."

Victor turned to me to see if I was listening. He seemed to like dramatic pauses. As he spoke, he would gesture broadly. Young Nog said later that it seemed as if Victor expected to be paid in latinum for each listener he convinced.

"About the time our ancestors were fighting through the dark ages," he said, including me, the chief, and Dr. Bashir in that statement, "the Mist were feeling crowded by the expansion of other races around them into space. The Mist of that time were a very private people who had no desire to expand beyond their own systems."

His use of the past tense bothered me, but I let him continue.

"Through a series of circumstances I'm not familiar with," Captain Victor said, "the Mist invented a device that simply shifts the molecular structure of all material slightly out of phase with normal matter. The shift is so slight that it almost can't be measured. The effect was that the shifted matter didn't exist in the normal universe."

"Not at all?" Nog asked, and then looked at me, as if I were going to chastise him for speaking. I did not even look at him directly, which, I believe, made him even more uncomfortable.

"Not at all," Victor said.

"Yet it's there," O'Brien said. "Completely invisible to those around it.

"So why can we see the normal universe," Dax asked. "And the shifted worlds can't be seen?"

"I honestly don't know the reason," Captain Victor said, "but I am sure one of our scientists could explain."

"Invisible systems and ships," Worf said.

Captain Victor said, "Not only invisible to those in the normal universe, but nonexistent."

"Thus the Klingon ship could pass through this ship," O'Brien said.

"And the effect we felt?" I asked.

"Simply a side effect of the fact that two bodies of matter are occupying the same basic space," said Victor. "Nothing more. And the Klingons felt nothing."

"We felt something," Sotugh said, *bregit* lung dripping off his fingers. "We have always felt something in that region of space. It is why we try to avoid it as much as possible."

"I know of the area of which you speak," said the small bristly alien. Until it spoke up, its snout had been resting on the chair's back. It had to lift its head to talk. "There are spacefaring legends of that sector. My people had strange dreams as they flew through that area. The Betazoids avoid it altogether. It makes them ill. Perhaps humans feel nothing, but it is not true of every species."

Around the room, a handful of others nodded. The Trill leaned back in his chair, a half-smile playing on his face. His gaze met Sisko's, and Sisko got the sense that the Trill was noting what he was: that it was becoming a contest among the patrons to see whose species was sensitive enough to "feel" the Mist.

Cap seemed to notice it too. And, like Sisko, he knew which way it was going to go. Add enough intoxicants, and every species reverted to childhood. Pretty soon, the entire thing would degenerate into a "my species is better than your species" brawl.

"So," Cap said loudly, effectively silencing the growing debate. "We know that Victor believed the Klingons felt nothing—"

Sotugh started to speak, but Cap continued—"even though we know that they did feel something. Then what?"

Sisko heaved a small sigh of relief. He was wondering how he was going to return to DS9 battered from a bar brawl and still convince Dr. Bashir that he'd rested.

"Well," he said, "I glanced up at the Klingon ship *Daqchov* floating near the Mist ship. Wouldn't they be shocked to know they were so close to another alien ship?"

"Shocked?!?" Sotugh said. "Klingons are not shocked. We are never shocked. We—"

"Sotugh," several patrons said at once.

The cat-woman finished the thought. "Would you kindly shut up and let him talk? How would you like it if someone continually interrupted your stupid operas?"

"They are not stupid," Sotugh said.

"Could have fooled me," the cat-woman said.

"Prrghh, Sotugh, please," Cap said. "The others want to listen to the story, not your bickering."

"That's what I was trying to tell him," the catlike woman, Prrghh, said haughtily.

"Then take your own advice, woman." Sotugh leaned back in his chair. "Continue with your lies, Sisko."

Sisko did not take the bait. He took another swig of Jibetian ale, and went back to the story.

Chief O'Brien looked as if the entire discussion was a revelation to him. "So that's why this area of space is so clear," he said.

Captain Victor nodded. "It has to be kept clear to cut down on episodes of the dizziness and dislocation that you felt."

"But the energy to maintain such a shift," Chief O'Brien said, "must be enormous."

Captain Victor shook his head. "Once shifted, the matter remains in that constant state unless purposefully shifted back."

Dax had a slight frown on her face. "When the planets shifted, the Mist would have had to shift everything. Air, food, water. Everything that sustained life, including the suns. I find that hard to believe."

"It happened," Victor said. "And more. The Mist called this the Great Move. Their history makes it clear that the shift was a gigantic undertaking that took years."

While I found all of this fascinating, and just vague enough to be confusing scientifically, I had other concerns. Many parts of this story made no sense, at least not with the things I could see.

"How did you shift into Mist space?" I asked.

Captain Victor laughed. "My ancestors ran into some problems near this area of space with their ship. The Mist saved the ship, as they have done with many other ships over the centuries. Many of my ancestors decided to remain on the Mist worlds. Like many other races, we have been accepted in their culture. I am now a tenth-generation member of the Mist community."

I made a small, noncommittal sound in the back of my throat. Dr. Bashir looked at me. He knew that sound was my way of continuing a conversation, but of letting my skepticism out.

"So," I said, "you claim the Mist have been completely out of touch with any other race, except for those members of those races that it has 'rescued.'"

I put quite an emphasis on the word *rescued*. I wondered if we had been "rescued" as well.

"Why would we be in touch with any other race? We opted to leave this part of space, to live in our own universe, so to speak," Victor said. "The affairs, the wars, of the normal universe do not affect us."

"Well," I said softly, "something must have affected you, Captain. You knew enough about our universe to lure us here."

"True," he said.

"And I suspect you would not have done so if your problem was restricted to your own space."

He smiled at me, but there was no laughter in the smile. And with that look I distrusted him even more.

"The Mist have no desire to expand," he said, "but we do have need of room for growth beyond our five systems."

"Oh," I said, not liking where this was heading.

Victor held up his hand for me to wait. "Two hundred years ago," he said, "we found another three systems that were uninhabited, in an area just beyond the Bajoran system. Since they were uninhabited, and no race seemed to be claiming them, they wouldn't be missed."

"You shifted them," Dax said.

"Exactly," Victor said. "We shifted the systems and began colonization."

"And you have had trouble with the colonies," Worf said. He sounded as coolly skeptical as I felt. Luring us away from *Deep Space Nine*, shifting us into their space, and then not giving us proper warning about the effect of the Klingon ship hadn't warmed any of us to Captain Victor.

63

Captain Victor glanced at Worf as if his question were rude. Worf glowered back, as only a Klingon can.

"We do not glower," Sotugh said.

Several patrons shushed him. Sisko suppressed a smile.

"It is a moody word," Sotugh said. "Klingons are not moody."

They shushed him again.

"Well," Sotugh muttered into his blood wine. "We are not."

Sisko forced himself to continue before he laughed. "It seemed that Victor did not like what he saw in Worf's face."

"Better," Sotugh said. "No human should like what he sees in a Klingon face."

"So," Sisko said, "Victor . . ."

. . . looked directly at me. "There were no troubles," he said, and then he sighed. It seemed as if some of the energy left him. "Until this last generation of colonists. Over half of the colonies' populations were made up of the descendants of ships like my ancestors. There are humans, Cardassians, Jibetians, Bajorans, and a dozen other races on those three colony systems."

"All living under the Mist system," Dax said, "but growing tired of the Mist rules."

Captain Victor nodded. "It would seem that way. Under the leadership of a human named John David

Phelps Jackson, the colonies have been demanding more and more."

I crossed my arms. "You brought us to help your side?"

Captain Victor shook his head. "Not really. We lured you here to get you, your fine crew, and your ship away from *Deep Space Nine.*"

I had not liked this conversation from the beginning, but now I hated it. I felt O'Brien stir behind me. Worf leaned forward on his console. Dax clenched her teeth, making her jaw seem quite firm.

Dr. Bashir took a step forward and asked the question we all were thinking. "And why would that be?"

"Because," Captain Victor said, "Jackson and the Mist colonists are about to shift *Deep Space Nine* into our reality and take it over."

"What?" I came up out of my chair. "They have no right to our station. *You* have no right to our station."

Victor stood calmly before the screen, as if he had expected my reaction.

"Of course we don't," he said.

I turned to Dax. "Is the station still there?"

"Yes," she said. "It's still in normal space, and still acting like we've gone missing. But . . ."

She bit her lower lip and looked up at Victor. The look she leveled at him should have caused him to quake in his boots.

"But?" Bashir asked. He, too, seemed unnaturally calm, something he had learned in his days on *Deep*

Space Nine. He had learned to mask the strong emotions—his anger—behind a veneer of calm.

"But," she said, "now I count twenty Mist ships taking up positions surrounding it."

I turned back to face Captain Victor. "It would seem," I said, "that by luring us here, you are helping them."

"Oh," he said, shrugging, "your presence on the station would have done nothing to stop the take-over." He sounded as if this sort of thing were routine.

Worf growled behind me. If I hadn't seen Victor's nervous glance at the commander, I wouldn't have realized that Klingons made him uneasy. But he went on as if he were fine.

"Imagine having twenty ships suddenly appear out of nowhere around your station."

"The station would be able to defend against twenty ships," Worf said.

"Maybe," Victor said, "but not as well with hundreds of men with weapons beaming in beside every member of your crew, before they had time to even react."

"Just as you beamed in here with our shields still up?"

"Exactly," Captain Victor said.

"They beam through shields?" Prrghh asked. "I hadn't understood that before."

"You should have been listening more carefully," Sotugh said, and belched loudly. He got up without excusing himself, moved around the end of the bar, and disappeared through the doorway leading to the bathroom.

"The captain mentioned it," the middle-aged woman at the bar said, "when Victor beamed in."

"I know," Prrghh said. "It's just the juxtaposition of details . . ." Then she smiled and held up the tiny glass of blue liquid she had been sipping from. ". . . or perhaps it is the nectar of Honeybirds." And then she laughed, a warm throaty sound.

Sisko smiled at her. He didn't feel as if he'd had too much Jibetian ale, although he could do with more than fruitnuts. "Do you have a kitchen?" he asked Cap.

"We serve some things," Cap said. "What would you like?"

"Let's see your bar menu," Sisko said.

"What about the story?" the bristly creature asked, lifting his snout off his chair.

"He was waiting for me," Sotugh said, adjusting his clothing as he walked. He was not walking quite straight.

"I am hungry," Sisko said.

"But the story—"

"I'm still thinking about beaming through shields," Prrghh said. "Can you do that, Sotugh?"

"Do you think I'd tell you if I could?" he asked and sat down heavily.

"What about your station?" the Trill asked. The question sounded more like a prompt than a need to know. "Did they take it over?"

"That's what we were trying to find out," Sisko said.

My crew, except for Dr. Bashir, were huddled over their stations, trying to discover exactly what was happening on *Deep Space Nine.*

"Captain," Dax said, her voice showing the worry she felt, "two Mist ships are shoving a large asteroid directly at the station."

"An asteroid?" I asked. I had not expected that. "How long until impact?"

"Two minutes and ten seconds," Dax said.

"Cadet, send a warning on all channels. See if you can send something slightly out of phase, if you can send a message from our reality to theirs."

"Captain, communications aren't really my—"

"Do it, Cadet. Dax, help him." I knew it was a long shot, but I wanted to try everything. "Chief, see if you can shift us back. We need to warn them. I will not just sit here while someone tries to destroy my station."

"Don't worry, Captain," Victor said in a voice that was much too smarmy for my liking. "The asteroid has been shifted into this reality. Its only function is to pass through the station."

"To disorient everyone," Worf said.

"Exactly," Captain Victor said. "After the asteroid passes through the station, they will shift the station and then beam in and take it over."

"Continue sending messages, Cadet. Chief—"

"I am, sir."

"I know," O'Brien said, huddled over his console.

"So," I said to Victor, "as far as any of the ships guarding the station, and the wormhole, are concerned, the station will suddenly disappear."

Captain Victor nodded.

I faced the Mist captain. "And just what do they plan to do with my station?"

Captain Victor shifted his gaze for a moment back to the viewscreen, then looked me right in the eye and said, "They plan on using it to conquer the Mist homeworld."

CHAPTER
7

"YOU HAVE NACHOS?" Sisko asked, interrupting himself as he stared at Cap's bar menu. "Chicago-style pepperoni pizza? Jambalaya? And dirty rice?" The selection was simply amazing. He was shocked.

The patrons around him groaned. "Captain, please, continue," the bristly alien said.

"And you have heart of *targ,*" Sotugh said, leaning over Sisko's shoulder. The smell of blood wine mixed with *bregit* lung was nearly overpowering.

"This is an extensive menu," Sisko said.

"Captain, please," the bristly alien said, slapping its fingered paw on the chair.

"If you see something you'd like, I'd suggest ordering it quickly," Cap said. "You don't want to see a Quilli get mad. At least not in here."

The bristles on the little creature were standing on end. "You have abandoned the story at a good section," it said, climbing on the slats of the chair's back.

The chair tottered precariously. "I demand that you continue."

"I will," Sisko said. Those bristles did look like quills, and if the Quilli could shoot them, like so many bristled creatures could, it would be bad. Very bad indeed.

"Now!" the Quilli growled.

"Are your nachos real?" Sisko asked Cap.

Patrons began moving away from the Quilli. Some ducked under tables. Others headed toward the door.

"Yes," Cap said, edging toward the bar, his gaze on the Quilli.

"Good," Sisko said. "I'd like a large."

"Captain, I demand to know what happened next!" The Quilli's bristles were trembling.

"What happened next?" Sisko said, looking at the small creature. Its chair was wobbling. The Trill got up and steadied it. The Quilli simply climbed higher.

"I put my entire staff on finding a way to get us phased into our own space."

"That's all?" The Quilli's little voice was rising.

"No," Sisko said. "That's not all."

"Keep broadcasting warnings," I ordered Dax and Nog. "Try anything. Chief, find a way to get a signal across."

My crew moved swiftly. I was furious. I took a step closer to Captain Victor. I wanted nothing more than to force him to return us to our home. But I knew his agenda was greater than that.

He looked amused. His blue eyes were twinkling, although he was not smiling. Not quite. "I'm afraid that you won't be able to get any signal between the two realities. Nothing crosses from this way to the normal universe. However, we can listen in on anything going on in the normal universe."

"Captain, I can't find the phase variance, let alone break it," O'Brien said. "Not in this amount of time."

"He's right, Benjamin," Dax said. "Miracles simply aren't possible at the moment."

I crossed the bridge. I stopped in front of Victor. He was my height, except for that silly yachting cap. I wanted to yank it off his head, but I didn't.

"Take us back," I said.

"Captain, really," Victor started.

"Take us back," I said again.

He shrugged. "If that's what you want, but warning your crew will only cause undue bloodshed."

"Shift us back. *Now.*"

"Fine." He took off the cap himself and stuck it under his arm, like those old nineteenth-century paintings of Napoleon. I almost expected him to put one hand in his shirt. "But if you want to come back across, simply return to this point and my ship will bring you here."

"We will not want to come back," I said.

"Don't be so hasty in your predictions, Captain," he said, and chuckled. Then he tapped his foot, and disappeared.

"That was a quick transport," O'Brien said.

"Maybe he was never actually here," Dax said.

"Check the logs later, people," I said. "Right now we have to warn the station."

At that moment a line in space seemed to form in front of the *Defiant,* widening and growing with a thin, white mist. It swept over the ship from front to back almost instantly and then was gone.

The Mist ship had disappeared.

"The Klingon ships and the station are hailing us, sir," Nog said.

Home. I hadn't realized how much I missed it. And yet I hadn't been out of sight of it.

"How long until the asteroid hits the station?" I asked.

"At the speed the Mist ships were pushing it," Dax said, "we have less than one minute. But I can no longer see it, or any of the Mist ships."

"Put the station on screen," I said. "Make sure the channel is secure."

"It is," Nog said.

"Secure, Captain," Dax said, at the same time, obviously double-checking the cadet on such an important order.

"Captain," Major Kira said as her face appeared on screen. "Where were you? We were——"

"Major," I said, "you have exactly thirty seconds before an attack on the station. Go to red alert. The first sign of the attack will be dizziness; then a hundred or so armed troops will beam into the station even though the shields are up. If you can't hold Ops, disable anything you can, especially shields and weapons. Do you understand?"

"Aye, sir," Kira said. She had already started to turn away, to issue orders, as the screen went blank.

"Dax," I said. "Move us two hundred meters closer to the station and hold that position."

Silence filled the bridge of the *Defiant* as I sat and stared at the screen.

"Captain," Nog said, breaking the silence. "The Klingons are insistent, sir."

"'The Klingons are insistent,'" Sotugh mocked. "Of course we were insistent. You appeared out of nowhere, in a position that we had just flown through."

"Shhh," the Quilli said.

Sotugh turned. Half the patrons ducked again. "Don't shush me, you pointed pipsqueak."

"You are interrupting the story," the Quilli said. Its bristles slowly rose.

Sisko wondered if he should duck. That small alien seemed to make most of the patrons nervous.

"I am part of the story," Sotugh said. "I want to make sure Sisko gets it right." He leaned over his chair and waved at Arthur, the kid behind the bar. "Where is my heart of *targ?*"

Arthur looked at Cap, who rose from the back bar, holding a blue bottle. "I don't recall you ordering any," Cap said.

"Of course I ordered some," Sotugh said. "When Sisko ordered his—neshos."

"Nachos," Sisko said quietly.

"The story!" the Quilli shouted.

"Did you know," the Trill said, crossing his arms and smiling, "that stories are the most important form of commerce on the Quilli homeworld?"

"Are you saying I'm trying to steal this one for a profit?" the Quilli snapped. Its bristles were shivering.

"Of course not," the Trill said. "I was merely explaining your insistence. Humans can be sloppy storytellers, especially when they're drinking. Sometimes they begin a story and never finish it. Sometimes they start in the middle and insist on an audience. Sometimes they tell a story that's too long for everyone to follow. With humans you never know what you might get."

"And sometimes they are filled with their own importance," Sotugh said.

"Are you saying," Sisko asked, slightly offended, "that I am a sloppy storyteller?"

"You do allow a lot of interruptions," the Trill said.

"If he were a better storyteller, there would be no interruptions," Sotugh said.

"You comprise the bulk of my interruptions," Sisko said.

"See? I am here to make certain of your accuracy," Sotugh said. "And obviously you are not accurate enough."

"He is a fine storyteller," the Quilli said. "In fact,

he is an excellent storyteller and the story is entertaining me. I object to the interruptions. I want them to stop."

"I don't think that's possible," the Trill said, "given the mixture of customers here." He smiled as he glanced around the table. "But then you should know that. How many stories do you leave here with, anyway?"

The Quilli whirled so fast that Sisko almost didn't see the movement. One bristle stuck out double the length of the others.

"Any more insults, Trill," the Quilli said, "and you will lose an eye. Is that clear?"

The Trill held up his hands. He did not stop smiling. "No harm meant."

The bristle slipped back into place. "None taken," the Quilli said. It turned back to its position. "Captain, I believe you had just gotten a message from the Klingons."

Sisko cleared his throat. "Yes," he said. "Right." He smiled impishly at his audience. "I had Dax put the Klingons on screen. Captain Sotugh appeared. He looked—younger—then—"

"Didn't we all?" Sotugh mumbled.

"—and quite dashing in his uniform."

"Enough of the flattery, Sisko," Sotugh said. "Go on with the story before the warthog decides to blind us all."

Sisko's grin grew. "You'll let me tell this part?"

"I am waiting for my heart of *targ*," Sotugh said.

"I take that for a yes," Sisko said. "Well, Captain Sotugh appeared on screen and said, without preamble . . ."

"Captain Sisko, we know you just sent a message to the station. What kind of trick is this? We demand to know what sort of cloaking device you are using."

"It is no trick," I said. "Train your sensors on *Deep Space Nine* and stand by."

"I cannot see why I—"

I told Nog to cut the communication, and he did. Now, remember, this is during that recent period of hostilities between the Federation and the Klingon Empire. I knew that I was taking a risk—

"Yeah, you know, I was wondering . . ." A chalk-colored alien rose from his spot against the wall. Sisko tried not to blink in surprise. He had thought the alien was a line of dirt until he moved. "If you had hostilities, how come you let one of their number on your ship?"

"Worf always was different," Cap said.

Everyone looked at him. Sisko wondered how he knew Worf.

"I don't care!" the Quilli said. "It's not relevant to the story. Will you please do something about these interruptions?"

"Actually, the question is slightly relevant," Sotugh said. "But of greater relevance is the risk that Sisko took in cutting me off. I followed his instruction—

any good commander would, just to see what kind of trick he was playing—but I also raised my shields and gave an order to power my weapons. If we had not seen—"

"What did you see?" the little creature was shaking with fury.

Sisko met Sotugh's gaze. "I'll take it from here," Sisko said softly.

"I think that's best," Sotugh said.

"The station disappeared," Sisko said. "Oh, not right away. First, Dax said . . ."

"The asteroid should be passing through the station right about now."

We knew what they were going through. I don't know about the others, but my ears rang in sympathy, my inner ear spun slightly, and a hint of dizziness returned.

It happened too quickly, and Captain Victor knew he had sent us back too late. I could only clench my fists and hope that my first officer, Major Kira, who had fought in more tight situations than the rest of us had seen together—with, perhaps, the exception of Dax—would find a way out of this one too.

And that was when the station disappeared.

"It's gone, Benjamin," Dax said softly.

The silence on the bridge was intense.

I sat for one moment.

One long moment, feeling more fury than I had felt since my wife died. Captain Victor had played us like we were his favorite violin. He had taken each string, plucking and plucking, until we became the melody he wanted.

The melody, the chords, the over- and undertones. We had been played, and he had known what he was doing.

I could see his smile as he beamed off our ship. *Don't be so hasty in your predictions, Captain,* he had said, and then he had chuckled.

Chuckled!

Knowing that his people were about to steal my station.

"Captain," Nog said. "The starships around the station are going crazy. There are more hails here than I've ever seen. And the Klingons are demanding to speak to you, sir."

I stood. I would take care of this, and then I would take care of the Mist.

All of them.

"Cadet," I said, "open a channel to all the Federation ships in the area of the station, and send this message directly to Starfleet headquarters. And patch in the Klingons."

"Yes, sir," Nog said after a moment of looking very fearful. I saw Dax bend over her instruments, and move a hand, helping him. Finally, Nog said, "Channel open, sir."

I took a step toward our screen.

"This is Captain Sisko on the *Defiant. Deep Space Nine* has been taken by a rebel group of the legendary people called the Mist."

I paused for a moment to let that surprising statement sink in to all who were listening. "My information on this takeover is limited, but as soon as I know more, I will send it to you on this channel. Please stand by."

I had Nog cut the broadcast.

"Sir, we are being hailed by everyone," he said.

I ignored that. I knew my statement would provide more questions than answers.

"Old man," I said to Dax. "Move us back to the coordinates where we came out of Mist space."

Dax nodded.

"We are going back over?" Worf said.

"Do you have any other ideas, Commander?"

"No, sir," Worf said. He scowled at his panel, then said, "But it is a trap."

"People," I said, glancing around at my bridge crew, "that band of Mist have just declared war on the Federation, whether they intended to or not. And we need the other band of Mist to help us get our station back."

"I don't believe we can trust them, sir," O'Brien said. "They want us to go back."

"The chief is right, sir," Bashir said. "If they truly wanted to prevent the capture of the station, they would have approached us sooner."

"Captain Victor is not to be trusted," Dax said.

"This is not a debate," I said, and my crew fell silent. But right at that moment I agreed with everything they were saying. I knew it was some sort of trap, I knew Victor couldn't be trusted, yet at that moment I had no choice if we were ever going to see *Deep Space Nine* in real space again.

"We're in position," Dax said.

As she finished her statement, a rift in space opened up. For the second time in one day, the Mist swallowed us.

CHAPTER
8

THE FIVE IMPOSSIBLE planetary systems had returned, and with them, the beautiful but deadly-looking Mist ship, with its arching wings and small main section. The shift was as disorienting as coming out of hyperspace for the first time. The mind cannot accept the difference: it knows where it was, and believes it should still be there.

I stood as we crossed through, wondering why we did not feel any real physical effects. Apparently Dr. Bashir wondered the same thing, for he frowned and took an empty console, quickly going to work.

Dax was watching the screen and the helm. The chief was monitoring the shift so that he might repeat it, working to figure out exactly what was happening.

I spread my legs slightly, bracing myself. I was tired of the games the Mist were playing. For the second time we had crossed into their space, and for the second time, I felt as if we were lured, even though this time it was my decision to come. The first time had been a rescue signal. The second time was *Deep Space Nine*.

Bait.

They had my station and I had gone for the bait. Yet they did not know what they had done. By taking the station they had left ships abandoned in space. They left the wormhole vulnerable, Bajor vulnerable. An entire section of space normally policed by the Federation was now open to attack from any and all sides.

We had to resolve this quickly, or there would be great loss of life—losses of a type that I couldn't even predict except that they would happen.

I wondered about the station: what was going on inside her. Kira and Odo could handle themselves. But what of Quark's and the other businesses on the Promenade? What was happening in the Bajoran temple and Garak's tailor shop? Had the Mist placed its troops all over the station or just in Ops?

I longed to know. I wanted to be both there and here, in order to fight properly.

"Captain," Dax said, "the station is now visible to us."

"And the Klingons are screaming at us, sir," Nog said. He sounded breathless.

At the moment, I did not care about the Klingons.

"We cared about you," Sotugh said. "You had vanished again. We thought that perhaps you were planning some sort of military maneuver."

The Quilli growled.

Sotugh ignored it, and leaned back, shouting, "Where is my heart of *targ?*"

"Coming, sir," Arthur said.

Sisko proceeded as if the interruption hadn't happened.

I did not look at the cadet. I had a rudimentary plan, and its key was timing. "Hail Captain Victor," I said.

"Yes, sir," Nog said.

"Chief, what have you learned?" I asked while I waited for Victor to respond.

"There's a lot of information here," O'Brien said, "but I'm not sure it's what I need."

"Figure it out," I said.

"Yes, sir," he said.

Then Nog said, "I'm putting Captain Victor on screen, sir."

Captain Victor's face filled the screen. He was grinning, his teeth impossibly white against his skin. He still had his cap off, and his dark hair was sticking up in tufts. Behind him, I could barely make out Councillor Näna, his strange face staring unblinkingly at me through his huge eyes.

"All right," I said. "We are back. But we are here to retrieve *Deep Space Nine.* I expect your assistance, and I expect it now."

"Captain," Victor said, spreading his hands. "We have done nothing but assist you."

"You have done nothing but play games with us," I said. "And the games are over. Now. The loss of *Deep*

Space Nine will cause a crisis of unparalleled proportions in the Alpha Quadrant. We must recover the station before word of this gets out."

"Too late," Sotugh said. "Word of it was already getting out. Within a minute of your second disappearance, I was picking up distress beacons from several ships."

Arthur swooped by with a platter heaping with nachos. The shredded beef smelled spicy. Jalapeños and black olives mixed with several cheeses and tomatoes on top. They were covered with homemade guacamole and real sour cream.

Sisko's mouth watered. He reached for a chip, then pulled back as the grease burned his fingertips. The nachos were too hot to eat.

"The story," the Quilli said, and tilted its chair toward Sisko.

"Oh, *relax,*" the Trill said, putting a foot on the chair's rung, and slamming it to the floor. The Quilli fell backward, its bristles sticking in the nearby tabletop, breaking its fall.

"On Quilla," it said, "you would die for that."

"On Quilla," the Trill said, "I would never do that."

Sisko sighed softly. He would have to wait a moment anyway to eat the nachos. He might as well continue.

"Where is my heart of *targ?*" Sotugh yelled.

"Coming," Arthur said, and scurried behind the bar.

"Captain Victor did not seem to care about the problems *Deep Space Nine*'s disappearance was causing in the Alpha Quadrant," Sisko said.

"I need to know what information you have about my station," I said to him, "and I need it now."

Victor's grin faded as I spoke to him. Apparently, in that instant, my return had ceased to be a joke to him.

He glanced at Nāna, whose head moved up and down in time to his opening and closing mouth. That seemed like a nod to me, but I might have been anthropomorphizing.

"We've intercepted some colonist transmissions," Victor said, smiling. "It seems the colony forces met with more resistance than they had expected and some of the station's equipment has been damaged."

They were fighting then. Trust the major to respond to such a command with quick, sure strokes.

"What kind of equipment?" O'Brien said, in a voice that had an edge of fatherly panic.

I raised a hand to silence him.

"My first officer responded quickly to my message," I said. I wanted Victor to know that my people were competent, even on the station. I still did not feel as if I could trust him. I wanted to warn him in as many ways as I could about provoking me.

"It seems to me that he had done a good job so far, and you had done nothing," Sotugh said. He reached for the nachos, pulled out one, and ate it, then spit it out. "Bah. Tastes like plastic field rations. How could you order this, Sisko?"

Sisko took a chip. The cheese formed a string as he pulled and he had to break it with his fingers. He licked them off. These were excellent nachos. He had ordered them because he was picky about his jambalaya. Now that he knew the nachos were a success, he might share them, and then order jambalaya.

"These are the best nachos I have had since I left Earth," he said to Cap.

Cap nodded. "We have a captain who comes in here regularly who loves them."

"Aren't you going to answer the Klingon's point?" the middle-aged man at the bar asked. "I kind of agree with him. I don't think you responded well to the challenge at all."

Sisko smiled. "I'm not a Klingon. I do not respond aggressively to every attack. I like to gather information first."

"It makes you seem weak," Sotugh said, craning his head for Arthur. There was still no sign of the heart of *targ*. Sisko wondered how long it would take before Sotugh got really upset.

"It makes you seem overly cautious," said the alien who had recently detached himself from the wall.

"It prevents costly mistakes," Sisko said, speaking around another beef-and-cheese-covered chip. He had gotten some guacamole this time, too, and it was fresh and extremely well made.

"I suppose we will have to wait for you to finish eating now before you continue the story," the Quilli said. It had freed itself from the table during the last bit of the story. It was sitting a little farther away from the Trill now.

"It is considered rude among humans to talk with their mouths full," the Trill said.

The Quilli shot him a nasty look. "It is not considered rude among Quilli."

"Well, then," Sisko said, pulling a large chip from the center, "I shall talk and eat. Unless there are other objections?"

"Please continue," someone said.

"Who cares about human customs?" someone else asked.

"It is rude for Klingons *not* to talk and eat at the same time," Sotugh said.

Sisko smiled and reached for the pile of napkins that Cap had set on his table. "I continued to ask Captain Victor for information," Sisko said, as he tried to pry yet another chip out of the middle of the nacho pile. "It seemed to me that if he were telling the truth, he was in as much trouble as I was."

"How is that?" the woman drinking tea at the bar asked.

"The Mist colonists would be using *Deep Space Nine* against him and his faction," Sisko said. "Victor had been, in his own way, proposing that we become allies. I was willing to accept that in the information exchange, but I was also listening closely, keeping an eye on him, and trying to make certain that what he told me matched what I saw."

* * *

"Your first officer's actions might buy us some time," Captain Victor said to me.

I hoped for more than time. I hoped that Kira would be able to subdue the invaders, and then we would be able to take the station back to our own space.

"What is your defense plan?" I asked.

Victor glanced at Näna. The councillor had moved away, and all I could see of his face was one large unblinking eye, set in his gray lifeless skin. "Our ships are not set up for fighting," Victor said. "We outnumber the colonist ships, but we would stand no chance against that station of yours."

"If you are not set up to fight," Worf said, "then what does it matter if you outnumber the colonists' ships?"

I had been about to ask that question myself, but it sounded better coming from Worf. Victor seemed startled by the question.

"I—we—can fight. Sort of," he said.

I resisted the urge to shoot a triumphant glance at Worf. "Sort of," I repeated. "What are you leaving out, Captain?"

Victor glanced in Näna's direction, but the councillor had moved completely out of our visual range. I could see only Victor's half of their interaction. He seemed worried.

"Captain," I said, my voice deep and filled with warning.

He turned back to me, his skin darkened by a flush. "The Mist are not a fighting people," he said. "For centuries, they have avoided conflict by simply not taking part in what they observed going on in the normal space around them."

"They hid," I said, feeling contempt mixed with a deep anger. I had a hunch I knew where this was going.

"Actually, yes," Captain Victor said. "And now they're faced with a conflict of their own making and most Mist simply won't fight."

"But humans will," I said, "which explains why you captain a Mist ship."

He nodded. "Contacting you was my idea. I felt that if we were going to win, we needed the help of those who knew how to fight."

"The Federation does not usually get involved in internal disputes," I said. "And when we do, we do so as a mediator. We do not take sides."

Unless forced to when one of our space stations was captured. But I did not say that to him. Not yet.

Victor's flush deepened. "But most Mist on the homeworlds simply want to let the colonists take over," he said, his voice rising in a forceful tone.

"Then perhaps that is what should be done," I said.

"No," Victor said. "You don't understand."

"Apparently not," I said.

He ran a hand through his tufted hair. "The colonists," he said, "don't share the goal of keeping the Mist reality and the normal space reality separate."

"What does that mean, exactly?" Worf asked.

But I knew already. I was beginning to understand. And so was Dax.

"It means that they have no qualms about phasing into our space and stealing a space station," she said to Worf.

"Exactly," Victor said. "That act of aggression against your station is only the beginning. Imagine the advantage a warlike group with the ability to shift anything, at any time, into this form of space would have."

"We'd have to develop whole new weapons to fight them," O'Brien said.

"We'd never see them coming," Bashir said.

"They could control this sector before we even knew what hit us," Dax said.

Captain Victor only nodded.

I didn't like Captain Victor and liked the message he carried even less.

"This is where you made your mistake," Sotugh said, shaking a goo-covered finger at Sisko. The heart of *targ* had been served while Sisko was talking, and Sotugh had eaten it quickly, scooping it with his fingers like a human child who hadn't been taught how to eat properly.

"And how is that?" the man at the bar asked.

Sotugh didn't even look to the questioner, but only at Sisko. "If you had become allies with the other faction, we would have that technology now. Imagine using it against the Dominion. Imagine going into the Delta Quadrant, phasing the Jem'Hadar into one area of space, and the Founders into another. They would never be able to find one another, and we would be free of them forever."

"Or we would have destroyed each other by now," Sisko said. "No one could keep secrets, since no one would know if a shifted person was nearby. For all we know, a Mist might be listening to this conversation right now."

"It would have to be a Mist captain," the Trill said with a twinkle in his eye.

"Provided Cap knew he was here," Prrghh said, and everyone chuckled.

"I am serious," Sotugh said. "It was a missed opportunity."

"At the time," Sisko said. "I did not recognize that the opportunity was there. I was concerned with *Deep Space Nine*. And what it meant that it was missing from normal space."

"Captain," I said to Victor, "are the colonist ships as unarmed as yours?"

"More or less," he said. "Over the last few years they have managed to install some weapons, but it was only a short time ago that we learned of their entire intent."

I stroked my chin as I thought. It was clear that we were going to need help. There were at least twenty colonist ships near the station. And if Kira hadn't gotten the station completely disabled, then the *Defiant* wouldn't be a match. Either way, we needed help.

And I still did not have enough information to formulate a plan.

I moved my hand from my chin, and let it fall at my side. I was standing at attention and I didn't even realize it.

"Captain," I said, "let me get this straight. You used your ship to bring us here, right?"

"Yes," Victor said.

"Can all Mist ships do that?"

"If they have the right technology," Victor said.

I nodded. I didn't like how this was shaping up. In any fight between ships from our space and the Mist, the Mist would win. All they had to do was use their technology to send us back to our own space. End of fight.

"So," I said, thinking of the shift that had just occurred with *Deep Space Nine,* "all the colony ships have the same technology, then, too."

Victor seemed to understand where I was going. "No," he said.

"No? But they kidnapped *Deep Space Nine.* Some of the ships had to have the correct technology."

"Some," Victor said. "Actually two."

"How do you know that?" Worf asked.

Victor smiled. "The secret of the technology is very closely guarded by the High Council. Trust me. Only two colony ships have the ability to shift objects."

I didn't trust him, but I said nothing.

"But why couldn't the colonists take the equipment apart, learn how it works, and just make more?" O'Brien asked.

"Because," Captain Victor said, "simply tampering with the shift device on board a starship causes the device to destroy itself. As I said, the High Council has guarded the secret carefully, and successfully, for thousands of years."

So my vision of a fight in which the ships from our space lost was not a correct one after all. "Well then," I said, "it seems we can safely go for help."

"For help?" Dax said. She looked at me as if she did not understand.

"You are thinking of going to the Klingons?" Worf asked.

I smiled at him.

"The Klingons are a very warlike race," Captain Victor said. "I'm not sure that would be a good idea."

I shrugged. "You need all the help you can get, and there's only one Federation starship close enough to do us any good."

"But I do not want to trade one problem for a worse one."

"Oh, you won't," I said. "As long as you can shift the Klingons and us back to normal space when this is under control. Sometimes you have to fight fire with fire."

Captain Victor nodded. "But I would prefer to not get burned."

Sotugh hit the platter of nachos with one hand and sent it clattering off the table. It landed on the floor, scattering nachos in every direction, and shattering the platter.

"You!" he shouted. "You set this up? You dragged us into your problem? Do you know what you did?"

"Denied myself some nachos," Sisko said, looking at the ruined meal longingly.

"This is not a joke, Sisko," Sotugh said.

The other patrons had backed away. Sisko hadn't moved.

"But it is long over," Cap said. He put a hand on Sotugh's shoulder. Sotugh threw him off, but to Sisko's surprise, Cap did not fall back. "Let the man finish his story."

"He is without honor. He does not deserve to tell stories!" Sotugh said.

"Oh, shut up," Prrghh said. "Let him finish. You might learn something. You can kill him when he's done." She smiled at Sisko, revealing small pointed teeth. "Tomorrow might be a better day to die."

"You mock me, Prrghh," Sotugh said.

"It's just that you're getting so tiresome, Sotugh," she said. "Can't you—?"

Sotugh jerked forward and let out a large groan of pain. He turned and pulled a bristle out of his buttocks. He held it up and shook it at the Quilli.

"I warned you, warthog—"

"No," the Quilli said. "I warned you. I want to hear the rest of this story."

"No one will hear the rest of it, if things don't settle down right now," Cap said.

"Oh, what can you do to us?" Prrghh said.

"Close the bar," Cap said.

"Close the bar?" Prrghh asked. "You've never closed the bar."

"I will, rather than have a fight between a Klingon

and a Quilli on the premises. Or a Klingon and a human." Cap looked meaningfully at Sisko and Sotugh.

Sisko leaned back in his chair. "I don't want you to close," he said. "Now that my nachos are gone, I'd like to try your jambalaya." Then he smiled. "And please put them on Sotugh's tab."

"You are pushing things, Sisko," Sotugh said.

"And you'd better clean that wound," the Trill said, "before the poison sets in."

"Poison?" Sotugh said, frowning at the Quilli. "Have you a med kit?" he asked Cap.

"In the bathroom," Cap said.

Sotugh shot a glance at the Quilli. "You and I will have business when we leave here."

"I'm willing to let it go if you allow Sisko to finish his story," the Quilli said.

"I'm not," Sotugh said, and stalked off to the rest room.

"Poison?" the middle-aged woman at the bar asked the Trill. "I'd never heard that Quilli bristles are poisonous."

The Trill grinned. "They're not. But that got him to shut up." He nodded to Sisko. "You can continue now."

The gecko climbed back up into Sotugh's temporarily vacant chair.

CHAPTER
9

"ALL RIGHT," Captain Victor said. "We shall bring the Klingons here." He turned to his crew.

I took a step closer to my screen. "Wait!" I said. I had a sudden image of the Klingons being brought into the Mist reality with no warning at all. They would have attacked first and asked questions later. "I need to warn them. You can't just bring them across."

"Captain, really," Victor said. "We brought you across with no warning, and you were fine."

He raised a hand.

"You said so yourself," I said quickly. "The Klingons are a warlike race. They won't respond as we did."

Victor's hand came down. He turned to me. "What do you suggest?"

"Send me back. Let me talk to them. I'll hail the Federation starship *Madison* as well."

Victor grimaced. "All right," he said. "But make it

short. I do not know how long it will take for the colonists to take control of your station."

Probably longer than you expect, I thought. But I did not say so. "We will return to these coordinates after I have spoken to them," I said.

Victor nodded. He was ready, and so was I.

Sotugh was standing near the bar. He had returned from the rest room during Sisko's last part of the story. "You were right," he said. "We would have attacked first, and then you would have had no hope of getting your station back. This is the first smart thing you have said all day, Sisko."

Sisko didn't know if he should thank Sotugh or ignore him. So he ignored him.

The line of Mist swept over the *Defiant,* and Captain Victor's ship instantly disappeared, along with the Mist homeworlds. *Deep Space Nine* and the Mist colony ships around it also vanished off our sensors as we returned to the normal universe.

I did not like this form of shifting, and I could tell that my crew did not either. Dax shook her head slightly as she looked at the console. Worf gripped the edges of his, as if steadying himself. Dr. Bashir actually rubbed his eyes as if he could make the images change.

"Captain," Nog said, "we are being hailed by the *Starship Madison,* sir."

"They are within range," Worf said. "I will be able to get them on screen shortly."

"And Captain," Nog said. "The *Daqchov* is demanding that you talk to them."

"I will speak to both of them at once, Cadet," I said. "Open a secure channel, and put both captains on screen."

I clasped my hands behind my back and waited as Nog completed my orders. I was secretly pleased that the *Madison* was the nearest starship. Captain Paul Higginbotham was an old friend of mine, and I knew how he would respond in battle. Captain Higginbotham was a judicious man who weighed all his options carefully and always seemed to make the proper choice.

"And what is your opinion of Captain Sotugh?" Prrghh asked, leaning near Sisko. "Aren't you going to summarize him for us as well?"

Sotugh frowned.

Sisko leaned back, closer to Prrghh, and said, "I don't think I have to. You all know Captain Sotugh. He is in battle much as he is here, opinionated and aggressive. Those are good traits for a warrior."

Sotugh lifted his mug of blood wine. "Well said, Sisko."

"And diplomatically, too," Prrghh whispered in his ear.

Sisko smiled at her, and then continued.

Captain Higginbotham was a tall slender man who perched in his commander's chair like a judge, hands templed before him as he contemplated me through the screen. Nog had split the images so that next to Captain Higginbotham, Captain Sotugh looked as if he might slash right through the screen at me.

"Captains," I said, holding up my hand to stop both of them before they could even speak. "We're in a situation that threatens both the Federation and the Empire and we have very little time to act, so if you'd wait until I've explained what has happened before you ask questions, it would help."

"It's your game, Ben," Higginbotham said.

"Your analysis had better be correct," Sotugh said, looking even more disgusted.

It took me less than two minutes to explain the situation with the Mist, the Mist colonies, and the reason *Deep Space Nine* had disappeared. I finished by explaining that the Mist colonists wouldn't stop with just taking over their own homeworld. The entire sector was in danger.

"Understand," I said, "that the information I have is through Captain Victor, and to be honest, I don't trust him. But I see no other choice."

"Had it been any other Starfleet captain telling me such a pack of wild tales, I would not have believed them," Sotugh said.

"Nonsense," Prrghh said. "I've heard that you once worked with Picard."

"Picard." Sotugh waved a hand in disgust. "Picard never explains anything to me. He simply expects me to follow him."

"Have you?"

"Followed him? No! We worked together at my direction," Sotugh said.

"That sounds like a story for another time," Cap said.

"Perhaps when we finish this one," the Quilli said, rubbing its front paws together.

"I won't tell a story so that you can sell it," Sotugh said. He crossed his arms. "Unlike Sisko here."

Sisko grinned. "May I continue?" he asked.

"Certainly," Sotugh said. "Go on. You are being surprisingly accurate at this time."

"Would it be fair to say that you were staring at me as if I were a crazy man when I finished?" Sisko asked.

"More than fair," Sotugh said. "I thought you were insane for saying these things, and I thought *I* was insane for believing you. Higginbotham, however, seemed to believe everything you said, no questions asked."

"Paul and I have served on some interesting missions together," Sisko said. "He knew that I would not lie to him or exaggerate anything, no matter how improbable."

"If those colonists have the station up and working," Higginbotham said, after I had finished, "it's going to take a lot more than two starships and three Klingon warbirds to stop them."

I nodded. I knew that. I also knew that our time was limited. The longer we delayed, the more critical the situation got in both phases of space.

"My people on the station only had thirty seconds'

warning before the attack," I said. "I have no idea how much time they bought us, but I do know they managed to cause some damage."

"If I had not seen your ship vanish and reappear so easily," Sotugh said, "and did not have the evidence of the space station disappearing, I would never believe such a wild story."

"Neither would I, Captain," I said. "But I have been to this phase of space twice now, and I need to go back. The threat is very real."

"I understand that," Sotugh said. "These 'Mist' may attack Klingon ships or the Klingon home-world. So we must act swiftly. We must not allow this technology to be used in such a dishonorable manner."

I knew that he was speaking not only to me, but to his crew and the other two Klingon warbirds.

Sotugh grinned. "Perhaps you should not tell stories," he said. "You are usually such a quiet man and we Klingons think that much misses you. But it is becoming apparent that nothing does."

Sisko raised his eyebrows. "Thank you," he said. "I think."

Sotugh took his seat again quickly, almost crushing the gecko, who barely snuck out from under him in time.

"I will be at your location in less than ten minutes," Higginbotham said. "The *Idaho* is thirty minutes away. Six other Starfleet ships are within an hour. I will notify them of the situation. But I have to warn you, Ben. I'm afraid the situation is going to get worse before it gets better."

"Cardassians?" I asked.

"I'm afraid so," Higginbotham said. "They have a fleet coming across the border, heading for the former location of *Deep Space Nine.*"

"The Empire is also sending ships," Sotugh said.

"Wonderful," I said. "Let's just hope in thirty minutes they won't be needed."

Captain Higginbotham and Captain Sotugh said nothing.

"Stand by, Captain Sotugh," I said. "Captain Higginbotham, rendezvous with us halfway between this point and the former location of *Deep Space Nine.*"

"Will do, Ben," Higginbotham said, and cut the connection.

"We stand ready to fight," Sotugh said.

"Thank you, Captain," I said, and signaled for Nog to cut the channel.

"Okay, people," I said, glancing around at my bridge crew. "Let's go get our home back. Dax, move us into position so that Captain Victor will know that we are ready."

"Yes, sir," Dax said.

A moment later a white line of mist opened in space and a thin cloud swept over first the *Defiant,* then the *Daqchov* and the other two nearby Klingon warbirds.

103

CHAPTER
10

"So, Sotugh," Prrghh said, leaning closer to Sisko and placing a tiny hand on his shoulder. "Is going through that barrier into Mist space like Sisko says?"

Sisko bent down to pick up a piece of glass from the broken plate that had lodged against the leg of the table. He then used that as an opportunity to move slightly away from Prrghh. He didn't know what her agenda was, but he suspected that if he allied himself with her in any way, he would make an enemy of Sotugh.

He and Sotugh had a bickering respect for one another. The last thing he wanted to do was lose that.

As he sat up, Sotugh's gaze met his. Arthur moved between them, picking up the empty heart of *targ* dish. He took the piece of glass from Sisko with a bit of a grimace. Arthur had worked hard during the last part of Sisko's tale to clean up the mess that Sotugh had made with the nachos.

"Well?" Prrghh purred.

"Sisko has described it accurately," Sotugh said.

"Suddenly," she said, "you seem quite reluctant to talk. Are you tiring of this, or do you think Sisko is being accurate?"

Sisko felt a flash of irritation, but he suppressed it as quickly as it flared. He asked Arthur to bring him some bottled water as well as another Jibetian ale when he brought the jambalaya.

Arthur nodded.

"Sotugh, you do not answer the lady," the wraith from the wall said.

"She is trying to make trouble," Sotugh said.

"But you have been making trouble all along," the wraith said.

"Not the kind Prrghh is making," Sotugh said. "She likes nothing more than disagreements among the people around her."

"So you do disagree with Sisko," the wraith said.

"I do not," Sotugh said. "I am listening to his part of the story. It gets tricky from this point on."

"That it does," Sisko said. He wiped his hands on a napkin, and leaned back. "Do you want to hear more?"

"Yes!" the patrons shouted in various tones and warbles.

To his surprise, Sotugh grinned at him. "It is a

successful story so far, Sisko," he said. "Do not keep your public waiting any longer."

Sisko smiled. "As soon as I saw the five improbable planetary systems . . ."

. . . and the beautiful Mist ship, its wings arcing darkly against the blackness of space, I had Cadet Nog open a secure channel to Captain Victor.

Within seconds of our arrival, Captain Victor's face appeared on the main screen. He had replaced his ridiculous little yachting cap, covering the tufts of his hair. It made him look like a young man playing games like Victory in Space. Behind him, Councillor Näna was almost completely visible. I didn't like the look of the councillor. Each time I saw him, he seemed no different, his gray scaly skin ghostlike, his eyes unblinking, and the mouth constantly opening and closing without saying a word.

After a quick glance at Näna, I addressed all my comments to Victor. "Before we go any further," I said, "I want to make certain that you can send our ship and the Klingon ships back to normal space at any time."

"At any time?" Victor repeated.

"Yes." I didn't want to explain myself any more than that, but I did want to be certain that the Mist could save themselves from us, as well as from the colonists.

"At the moment, we can," he said. It was a hedge, but a small one. Dax glanced at me. There was a

warning in her eyes that I didn't completely understand. But before I could say anything, Victor continued. "We will bring over the *Starship Madison* at the
point you designated to meet it."

"Good." I glanced at Nog. He was monitoring
everything. He seemed to have grown more mature,
just in the space of this mission. "Hail the *Daqchov*.
But keep this channel secured."

Nog worked for a moment; then the main screen
split, showing both Captain Victor and Sotugh.
Sotugh looked slightly disoriented.

"Ah," Sotugh growled. "This is where your per-
ception is incorrect. You were disoriented upon
your arrival in Mist space. I was merely gathering
data."

Sisko suppressed a smile. "My mistake," he said.
"Captain Sotugh looked as if he had been hastily
gathering information."

"I don't care how he looked," the Quilli said.
"What happened next?"

"I introduced Captain Sotugh to Captain Victor
and Councillor Näna," Sisko said.

"And in this Sisko was not exaggerating," Sotugh
said. "Näna was one of the most disgusting aliens I
had ever seen. But I did not say so at the time. I was
too intent on the mission at hand."

"In fact, he began the communication by insulting
me," Sisko said, his smile widening.

* * *

"Sisko," Sotugh said, "I see you were not lying. But retaking your station with five ships is an idea of a fool."

The Klingons were never polite, not even when we were allies. But Victor seemed taken aback by Sotugh's words. I did not try to soothe him. Instead, I stood my ground, which was always the best course with Klingons.

"True enough," Sotugh muttered.

"I hope you have a plan," Sotugh said.

"Of course I do," I lied. I had the beginnings of a plan, but not a full-fledged one. Not yet. "While it is true that five ships aren't enough to take a space station, I am assuming that Captain Victor and his forces will help, since they have an interest as well."

"It still seems risky," Sotugh said.

"I thought Klingons liked risk," I said.

"We calculate risk just like you do, Captain," he said. "Only we act upon it differently."

"I figured you would help with this fight."

"And I will," Sotugh said. "We seem outnumbered."

"Perhaps," I said. "But Captain Victor has stated that the colony forces are limited."

Victor had been watching our exchange with increasing nervousness. He clearly feared the Klingons.

"A healthy and wise response," Sotugh muttered.

* * *

"Their forces are limited," Victor said. He tugged on the bill of his cap, securing it on his forehead. "But we must be careful. You must not destroy the two ships with the ability to shift objects from the main universe."

This was news to me, but it was Sotugh who asked the question, or rather, barked it.

"Why?"

Captain Victor glanced nervously at Councillor Näna. Näna's mouth opened and closed, he did not blink, and yet Victor seemed to have gotten something from the exchange. He said, "Only the same instrument that shifted the station into the Mist space can shift it back to normal space."

I froze. I did not like the way that Victor played these games. "Let me get this straight," I said. "You're saying that if your ship is destroyed, the *Daqchov,* the *Defiant,* and the other two Klingon ships will be stranded in this space."

"That is correct, Captain."

"And if we destroy the ship that shifted the space station it will remain shifted," Sotugh said. He sounded as if he were contemplating the idea.

"That also is correct," Captain Victor said.

I didn't like the look on Sotugh's face, but I did not challenge it at that time.

"Sisko," Sotugh said, "you are suggesting that I would intentionally destroy the colony ship that shifted the station."

Sotugh seemed unnaturally calm about this accusation. Sisko slid his chair slightly farther away from Prrghh's. The bar was quiet. The others seemed to think that Sotugh was upset.

Sisko smiled. "Of course I am," he said. "It would have been a brilliant move. If you destroyed the ship and stranded DS9, you would have, with one blow, made quite a difference in any conflict with the Federation. We would have lost—permanently—a very valuable and strategic asset."

"True," Sotugh said. His eyes twinkled. He *had* thought of it. Sisko kept his own expression neutral as Sotugh continued. "But at the time I felt the station would be more of a threat to the Empire in the hands of the Mist. I did not as yet know that would not be possible."

Sisko shrugged. "It's my story. And, at the time, I thought what I thought."

"It seems logical," the middle-aged man at the bar said.

Sisko nodded slightly in his direction. But Sotugh frowned. He did not seem to like the fact that someone else agreed with Sisko.

"What would you have done in my position if our roles had been reversed?" Sotugh asked.

Sisko raised his bottle of ale with a slight smile. "I would have considered destroying the colony ship that had shifted the station."

"We are more alike than you like to acknowledge," Sotugh said.

"I thought you were the one saying we were different."

"Only at the beginning of the battle, Sisko," Sotugh said. "Only at the beginning."

This new wrinkle had me very disturbed. Suddenly, we had no margin for error. "Captain Victor," I said, "how can we tell which two colony ships are the ones with the ability to shift?"

Again Victor glanced at the councillor. The councillor's mouth continued to open and close. One of his eyes shifted slightly as if it were looking at Victor, and then shifted back, all unblinking.

That seemed to mean something to Victor. He said, "There is no way to tell, but the ships with the shift modules won't have weapons. Most likely they will back away from any fight."

"That is not good enough," Sotugh said.

I agreed, but did not say so. I wanted as much information as I could gather. I did not want any more surprises.

"What kind of weapons are we facing with the colony ships?" I asked.

"Actually, Captain," Victor said, "our intelligence tells us that only two, maybe three of the colony ships have been outfitted with any sort of weapons. But neither of them would be a match for one of your ships. It was the firepower of the station the colonists were gambling on getting."

"Then let us hope Major Kira managed to disarm the station's weapons," I said. "Is there anything more you need, Sotugh?"

"We are ready to fight," Sotugh said.

I nodded. "We take Ops first. From there we can control the rest of the station."

"Understood," Sotugh said, and cut his communication.

I had Nog cut the communication, then I said, "Set course for *Deep Space Nine,* warp factor five."

"Yes, sir," Dax said. "We'll be there in exactly twelve minutes."

As we turned and jumped to warp, O'Brien said, "I don't like this."

"Neither do I," Nog said.

"What is there to like?" Worf asked.

I sat down. Sometimes I could learn a lot by listening to the digressions of my crew.

"There's just something odd going on with Captain Victor," O'Brien said. "Something he's not telling us."

"He hasn't told us a lot of things," Dax said. "And I would guess that much of what he has said is lies."

"And we will deal with that," Worf said. "But first we must recapture the station. That is our first priority."

Dr. Bashir had been quiet through all of this, studying the screen and the console before him. Finally he looked up. "Doesn't it strike anyone else odd that five systems full of people, plus another three systems full of colonists, have existed in this region for centuries and none of them have ever turned up outside of legend?"

"You have a good point, Julian," Dax said. "I have early memories of the legends about the planets of the Mist disappearing. But I don't remember hearing anything about someone meeting their race. Nothing but legends."

Bashir was tapping his console. "I don't like the way these things are adding up," he said. "I have a few facts from my console, and I know the chief does as well. Combine that with this lack of information, and I think there may be more to this shifting than we're initially seeing."

I didn't entirely follow Dr. Bashir's logic, but then he often left out crucial details when he was thinking aloud. It led, in the early days, to people underestimating him around the station. I had not underestimated him in years. His hypotheses usually had some basis in fact.

"Check it out," I said.

Bashir nodded and quickly left the bridge.

"There's going to be a crowd waiting for us," Dax said.

I could see what she meant. At least twenty Mist colonist ships surrounded the station. Among them were twenty or so vessels in normal space that had been docked to the station or in orbit around the station when it vanished.

On top of that, a half-dozen unaligned Cardassian ships, privateers not part of their regular fleet, were approaching and would arrive at the station just minutes before we did. Attacking the station was going to take running an obstacle course first.

"You could have warned us, Sisko," Sotugh said. "Obstacle course indeed. More like a gauntlet of pain and dizziness. Do you know what happens to Klingons when they get dizzy?"

"I bet it improves their disposition," Prrghh said sweetly.

"So you and the Klingons went through that obstacle course?" the Quilli asked, resting its paws on the top of its chair.

Sisko smiled at it. When it got its story, it was actually quite a charming creature. "We did," Sisko said. "But Sotugh has jumped a bit ahead of our story."

"Don't get that warthog mad at me again," Sotugh said. "I didn't do anything wrong this time." He rubbed his left buttock absently as he spoke.

"Ah, that's right," the Quilli said. "The *Madison* isn't there yet."

Sisko nodded. "But it was just a half second later that Dax reported . . ."

"The *Madison* has shifted and joined us." She bent over her console, fingers working rapidly. "We'll be at the station in five minutes."

"Sir!" Nog said. "Captain Higginbotham is hailing us."

"Put him on screen," I said.

Captain Higginbotham's serious face filled the

screen. "What an amazing place you found here, Ben."

"It is startling, isn't it?" I said.

"What's your plan?"

"We're going in to take Ops first."

"It's going to get crowded in there," Higginbotham said. "Fighting in such close quarters is not going to be easy."

"Granted," I said. "Avoid passing through a ship in real space."

"You can do that?"

I nodded. "And it's not pleasant. Most of the colonists' ships are supposedly unarmed, but I don't trust that information. The biggest problem we have is we can't let any of the ships escape, and unless they fire on us, we can't destroy them, either."

"That's unusual," Higginbotham said. "What's the idea behind that?"

"It's complicated, Paul," I said. "But in abbreviated terms, we think we need the colonist ships with the transfer equipment to shift the station back, or it's stuck here, invisible, forever."

"Does that affect us as well?" he asked.

"Yes," I said, and told him about Victor's ship.

"Got it," Higginbotham said. "We'll back you up and keep as many of the Mist ships rounded up as we can."

"Thanks," I said, and had Nog cut the communication.

"Captain Victor's ship is dropping back," Dax said. "And being joined by half a dozen other Mist ships."

"I did not expect to see more Mist ships," Worf said.

"Me, either," Nog said.

"He mentioned them," O'Brien said uncertainly.

"Are they joining us?" I asked Dax.

Dax shook her head. "We're out here alone, Benjamin. It's just the three Klingon ships, the *Madison,* and us."

"I don't like this," O'Brien said to himself.

Right at that moment, I completely agreed. Something felt wrong. Very wrong.

CHAPTER
11

MY HEART WAS POUNDING as I leaned forward in my chair. It seemed as if I had already been in battle, judging by my body's reaction. I knew that I had to be prepared, and already I was on alert.

"Worf," I said, "I need to know the status of the station as soon as you can give it to me."

"Aye, sir," he said.

"We'll be in scanning range within one minute," Dax said. "The *Madison* and one Klingon ship are taking positions between the station and the colonists' home planets."

"Are the station's shields up?" I asked as we dropped out of warp.

"Shields are down, sir," Worf said. "Cardassian ships, led by Gul Dukat, have stationed themselves near the wormhole."

I expected as much. From Gul Dukat's point of

view, the station was gone. That meant the wormhole was up for grabs. Dukat was going to be in for a large shock when the station suddenly reappeared.

"We'll worry about Dukat later," I said. "Right now, we concentrate on regaining the station."

"Captain," Worf said. "I am reading phaser fire in a dozen places around the station, including Ops."

Dax smiled. She knew, as I did, how difficult the station would be to take. Months later, it would take the Dominion and the Cardassians working together to capture *Deep Space Nine*—after a long and difficult struggle. The colonists did not have that kind of force.

"You don't have the station anymore?" Arthur asked from behind the bar. He was cleaning glasses. Sisko wondered what happened to his drink and jambalaya orders.

"Oh, I do," Sisko said. "The struggle with the Dominion and the Cardassians is another story, and believe me, I do not have time for that one even if I were to quit telling this one now."

"Don't quit," the Quilli said.

The Trill grinned, and cast a sidelong glance at the Quilli. "It might be dangerous for all of us."

The Quilli frowned at him, its bristles moving forward with the furrowing of its tiny brow. "I'm not always violent," it said. Then it climbed on the back of its chair. The chair tottered precariously. "I wouldn't mind hearing the Dominion story after this one, though."

"Greedy bastard," the middle-aged man at the bar said just loudly enough for everyone to hear.

Sisko held up a hand. "I'd love to tell it," he lied. "But I don't think my voice will hold out that long." He held up his empty ale bottle. "When's my refill coming?"

Arthur blushed. "I thought you wanted it with the jambalaya," he said.

"You're cooking the jambalaya from scratch, aren't you?" Sisko said. Somehow he had expected them to have it on the stove, waiting. "I think I'd better have the ale now. And the water."

"It won't be long for the food," Cap said.

"Still," Sisko said. His voice was rasping against his throat. He still had a lot of story to tell, and with this crowd, it wouldn't do to run out of voice before he ran out of story.

"Coming right up," Cap said.

Sisko nodded, and then cleared his throat. "As I was saying—"

"Dax had smiled," the Quilli said breathlessly. Sisko was shocked at its memory. It grinned—a shaggy, toothy smile—and put its paws under its chin, bracing itself. "She knew how difficult the station was to take—"

"And on and on," the Trill said.

The Quilli ignored him. "The colonists didn't have that kind of force. Over to you, Captain."

"Um," Sisko said, still slightly shocked. "Right. Um. Oh, yes . . ."

* * *

"Our people are still putting up a fight," O'Brien said, his voice excited.

I had done the right thing, leaving Kira in charge. She could defend the station with sticks and rubber bands if she had to. I was as pleased as my crew was at the news of the continued fighting.

"Now we must help them," I said. "Dax, you have the bridge. Help the *Madison* keep those Mist colony ships in a tight group. Worf, Chief, you're with me."

Without another word I turned and headed for the transporter room. I wanted my people to beam into the station before the Klingons had a chance to get there.

"What did you think we would do, Sisko? Join forces with the Mist?" Sotugh wiped the blood wine off his mouth with the back of his hand as he spoke.

"No," Sisko said. "But I had a balancing act. I had to remember that in our space, you and I were on the verge of total war. It wouldn't do to have Starfleet troops running around the Empire at that time, would it?"

Sotugh scowled. "Point taken," he said.

We had just reached the transporter room when Dr. Bashir joined us. I had seen him in many states over the years—from a green doctor on a far station outpost to one of the most skilled, and calm battlefield surgeons—but never before had I seen him look like this. His angular face was white with shock. He looked both determined and angry.

"What is it, Julian?" I asked.

He scanned us. His gaze stopped for a moment on the transporter operator, a young Vulcan who was fresh out of the Academy. She nodded at him, her features impassive. He turned away.

"I found one of the items that Captain Victor failed to mention," he said.

I did not like the sound of this. It was something large enough to distress Dr. Bashir. "Make it quick, Doctor. We must get to the station."

"'Quick' is the operative word, Captain," Bashir said. "If we stay in this altered space longer than two hours and six minutes, we won't ever go back to our own space."

"Not ever?" O'Brien asked.

The three security officers I had sent for while we were on the turbolift arrived. They looked at all of us as if our very expressions were alarming. I held up a hand to them, and they waited.

"Not ever," Bashir said.

"How can that be?" I asked.

"Matter alters in this space," Bashir said. "The shift changes the property of matter in such a fashion that it can never be shifted back. Us, the station, the Klingons. Everyone."

"Our molecular structure is changing?" Worf asked with a tone of complete disgust.

"That's right," Bashir said. "And according to my

calculations, the change will be irreversible in a little over two hours."

"Two hours and six minutes from our last shift."

"Exactly," Bashir said. "And not one moment longer."

"So that's why no one sees the Mist," said the Caxtonian at the bar.

Sisko jumped. He had known the Caxtonian was there—Caxtonians were hard to miss, what with their incredible body odor and forceful opinions—but this one had been silent until now.

"Right?" he asked.

Sisko nodded. "That, in fact, was what clued Dr. Bashir into the problem in the first place."

"That's right," the Quilli said. "He mentioned something about it on the bridge."

"And then he started to investigate it," Sisko said, "and he came up with this."

"I hear that Bashir is abnormally intelligent," Sotugh said.

"More blood wine?" Arthur said, holding another mug. Sotugh looked up. Sisko was glad for the distraction. He didn't want to answer that question.

"Yes," Sotugh said, taking the mug.

"After hearing that news," Sisko said, starting into the story quickly so that Sotugh couldn't say anything more. "I realized we had a lot to do and very little time in which to do it. Because if we had two hours in which to act, the station, which had crossed over earlier, had even less time. And they didn't know it yet."

"Are you absolutely certain?" I asked him.

"I double- and triple-checked my figures," Bashir said. "I'm quite certain."

I got on the transporter pads and signaled the rest of my team to join me. Worf was already on his. O'Brien climbed to the platform, followed by the three security officers who were, I must say, looking quite confused.

"I wouldn't push the time limit if we can help it," Bashir said. "My figures are accurate, but I'm not certain how the gradual shift will affect us if we cross back to our space, say, two hours and four minutes from the point of shift."

"Are you saying that it could be painful?" O'Brien asked.

"He is saying that it might kill us," Worf said.

"Or it might make us wish we were dead," one of the security officers said.

"Actually," Bashir said. "It's more like trying to go through water that is slowly turning to ice. I doubt it will harm us, but one should be careful."

"I see your point, Doctor," I said. "We will hurry. How much time do we have?"

"If we're going to save the station," Bashir said, "we have one hour and ten minutes. The *Defiant* and the Klingons have about twenty minutes longer, thanks to that last visit back to normal space. The *Madison* a little longer."

"All right." I nodded at Bashir. "Excellent work, Doctor." Then I looked at the transporter operator. "Beam us into the middle of Ops."

"Aye, Captain," she said, and started the transport.

Sisko paused. The spicy scent of jambalaya made his stomach rumble. Arthur came out of the back, carrying a large bowl in one hand. The bowl was steaming. In the other hand, he held silverware. He set the bowl down in front of Sisko.

Sisko's mouth watered. There, mixed with the rice (which was properly browned before someone added the liquid), were pieces of ham, pork, and authentic Creole sausage. He picked up his fork and pushed the food apart, locating fresh shucked oysters. He had no idea how Cap had found those on Bajor, but he didn't care.

He forgot the story; he forgot everything else. It had been a long, long time since he'd had an authentic jambalaya. He scooped some rice and sausage onto his fork, and brought it to his mouth. He was about to taste it when Prrghh said,

"Well?"

He sighed and set the fork down. "Well, what?"

"Did you get to the station or will we be forever stuck in transport?"

He was tempted to say that they all died in transport, their molecules scattered to the seven seas—or

some appropriate metaphor. Instead, he gazed longingly at his jambalaya and said,

"No. We arrived in the middle of a firefight."

Smoke filled the air. Dozens of small fires burned
under and near panels. Ops had been clean and well
lit and in prime condition when I last saw it. Now it
was dark and filthy and littered with smashed equipment.

We had arrived in the very center of Ops. In case I
didn't tell you, our Operations area is built in a
sunken circular pattern, and we were in the middle of
that sunken circle. Although I knew there were others
in the room, I could not see them, except as shadows
in the smoke. O'Brien, proprietary as always about his
engineering work on the station, made a small sound
of dismay at the mess, but that was the only reaction
we were allowed.

A phaser shot cut between me and Worf, spinning
one of the security officers around behind me. The
chief and I ducked behind Kira's station as Worf
rolled to a position under the security panel. The
other two security-team members dragged the injured officer to a sheltered position near Dax's station.

"Good to see you, Captain," Major Kira's voice
rang out over the craziness.

"Good to be seen, Major," I said.

More phaser fire cut into the panel near my head,
scattering metal. One piece stuck into Worf's arm, but

he didn't seem to notice as he returned fire, sending a colonist twisting up and backward in pain.

Through the smoke, I did my best to get a grasp on the situation. It seemed that Kira and three others were pinned down against the wall near the turbolift by a dozen Mist colonists near my office. But, from the looks of things, she had made sure that even if the colonists had captured the station, it wouldn't be working for a time.

I tapped my comm link. "Dax?"

"Go ahead, Captain."

"Lock on to the life signs nearest my office and beam them into the brig."

"Aye, sir."

For a moment the firing continued; then suddenly it stopped as the Mist colonists were beamed away. It took a moment before Kira and her group realized it was over.

"That's it?" Kira said, standing up. "That's it? Beam them away and it's all over?"

She sounded almost disappointed.

"No, Major," I said. "This stage is over. We still have a long way to go."

"Boy, do we," O'Brien said, brushing some dirt off himself, and staring at the mess.

Dax's voice came clearly over the now silent room. "Captain, we have six colonists in the brig. The Klingons have beamed onto the Promenade and are taking care of the remaining colonists there."

"Good," I said. "Beam Security Officer Thomason

to sickbay. Stand by to beam me back to the *Defiant*'s bridge."

"Aye, sir," Dax said.

Thomason became a series of light-colored particles, and then vanished. Worf moved a piling aside. The other security officers began putting out the fires. O'Brien found the environmental controls and brought the lights back up.

That was a mistake. The edges of the smoke reflected the light, while the interior sucked the light inside. My eyes felt as if someone had rubbed them raw.

Then the exhaust fans started, gathering the smoke and sending it through long vents toward the vastness of space.

I felt an internal clock ticking away. We didn't have much time. I turned to Worf. "Secure this area and set up a guard. Be prepared for any beam-in attacks."

"Yes, sir," Worf said, quickly turning and directing the remainder of Kira's crew and the two security-team members to positions.

"Chief," I said, "you and Kira need to get this place back up and running as quickly as you can."

"That might not be so easy," Kira said. She pushed a strand of hair out of her face. She was covered in soot. Two long gashes had nearly severed the sleeve of her uniform.

"I understand," I said. "But do what you can. I plan to make this station reappear in the middle of all those Cardassian ships. In the very least, I would like to have shields. Ideally, I would like weapons to go with them."

"We'll see what we can do, sir," O'Brien said.

"At least we sabotaged them," Kira said. "We know how we broke them. We should know how to fix them."

"It's easier to break things than it is to repair them," O'Brien said.

They continued bickering—which was sometimes their best work method—as I beamed out of the station. In those few seconds between leaving the station and arriving on the *Defiant,* I felt hope. Hope that we could accomplish the goals we set out to accomplish. Hope that we would make it back.

But the moment I materialized on the *Defiant,* that hope vanished. It seems that there were a few more things about the colonists and this entire situation that Captain Victor hadn't told us. If Dr. Bashir was right, it looked as if the station was never to leave Mist space.

"And I," Sisko said with a grin, "am going to have a bite of this jambalaya if it kills me."

"It very well might, Captain," the wraith said.

"You can't stop there!" the Quilli said. "What did you see?"

"Let the man eat," the Trill said. "The last thing you want him to do is pass out from hunger."

"I could finish this," Sotugh said.

Sisko ignored them all. His taste buds were enjoying the perfect blend of rice, meat, butter, and vegetables. Cap had done the spices exactly right—just enough cayenne and chili powder, and the all important cloves.

He sighed in gastronomic ecstasy as all around him, the patrons of the bar began pounding their fists on the table and bar, demanding that he continue with his story about the Mist.

CHAPTER
12

"SILENCE!" Sotugh said, standing up. He held his hands out, palms down, as if he were directing an orchestra to play its music softer.

The patrons stopped pounding, but their hands or paws or limbs rested on the edge of the tables, waiting.

Sisko took advantage of the moment. He hadn't realized how hungry he was, or how long it had been since he had had any jambalaya besides his own. This was wonderful. And it went very well with Jibetian ale.

"I will tell you about the fight for the Promenade," Sotugh said.

"No!" several voices yelled.

"We want to know what Sisko saw!"

"What happened next?" the Quilli was standing on the very back of its chair. The Trill had his booted foot resting casually on the chair's seat, so that it wouldn't tip over.

Cap crossed his arms and leaned against the bar. He was grinning. "You have them, Captain," he said.

"Suspense is good," Sisko said around a mouthful of food.

"But not always the best for my bar," Cap said. "I promise you, the jambalaya will remain warm."

Sisko sighed, swallowed, and pushed the bowl away. Around him, patrons applauded, and the little Quilli fanned its bristles in joy.

"What I saw," Sisko said, and stopped, his throat closing around the words. The very thought of the destruction angered him to this day.

"What I saw," he began again, softer, and to an audience that was leaning forward in anticipation, "seemed as strange to me as those impossible planets had when I first entered Mist space."

"Was everyone dead?" the middle-aged woman at the bar asked, breathlessly.

"On the ship, no," Sisko said. "But in space—" He shook his head. "In space, the destruction was indescribable."

The first words I heard were Dr. Bashir's. He was standing at his console, near the command chair, where Dax had beamed me aboard.

"I can't believe it," he said, and if anything, he looked even more shocked than he had when I had first left the *Defiant*. I couldn't believe that he wasn't already in sickbay. I had beamed the injured security officer to him not a few moments before.

I frowned at him, and was about to say something,

when I realized that everyone on the bridge was staring at the screen.

I turned.

And felt all of the breath leave my body.

Let me try to explain this, for what I saw was a jumbled mess that at first made no sense to me at all. It took almost a half a minute for my brain to process the images.

Deep Space Nine remained in its normal place. That, as I have told you before, was how it looked from Mist space. Around it floated Cardassian ships, the handful of other ships that had been at the station when it disappeared, and, of course, the wormhole. All in normal space.

At first glance, this was what I saw, because this was what I expected to see. This was what I always saw when I was in the *Defiant* near *Deep Space Nine*.

"Minus the Cardassian dogs," Sotugh said.

Sisko nodded in his direction. "That's right," he said. "They would not normally be near the station unless there was trouble."

And believe me, I processed their presence that way: as trouble. To the Cardassians, of course, the station was gone, and they were guarding the wormhole. The approaching Klingon fleet would surely challenge that idea. A dozen other ships from different races were holding off toward Bajor, waiting.

That was what I expected to see, and what I did see.

It was in Mist space where everything had gone wrong.

Sisko cleared his throat. This was hard to say. He took a swig of Jibetian ale and that didn't help. Finally he downed half the bottle of water, wiped his mouth with the back of his hand as Sotugh had done, and looked at the other patrons. They watched his every move.

"Oh," he said when he regained his voice, "the *Madison* was still there, and the Klingon ships . . ."

. . . but the Mist ships had been destroyed.

Completely.

Imagine twenty of those lovely Mist ships, the wings arched over the small bodies, black against the darkness of space. Then imagine them shattered, those black pieces shrapnel, space debris, junk, floating and twisting in a grotesque imitation of dance. The pieces spun all over space, going through—at least to my eyes—the Cardassian ships, spinning out of control toward the wormhole.

I sank into the command chair.

All the hope that I had held, all the feelings that I had had, the beginnings to the end of this nightmare, were gone. *Deep Space Nine* would now be forever a part of Mist space. That was what I thought at that moment.

The implications were incredible: there would be a war for the wormhole. The Klingons and the Cardassians and the Federation, not to mention Bajor, and of course, the Dominion—although at that time I had no idea of the scope and power of the Dominion—would all battle for this small sector of space. Kira, Odo, and the others would have to remain here, in this strange reality, for the rest of their lives.

"But that didn't happen," the wraith said. "You've talked about the station since."

"Shhhh," said everyone around him.

I said nothing to the doctor. I knew that he had already thought of this implication. That is why he looked even more shocked than he had before.

What I first needed to know was who made this tragic error—and then I needed my best medical and engineering minds on finding a way to get my station back to its proper place in space, before that sector of space became a battleground.

"What happened?" I asked. My voice felt as if it had come out of a deep well.

"I've never seen anything like it," Dax said, and in her voice I could hear the same shock that I felt. "Two of the ships tried to make a run past the *Madison*."

"*Paul* did this?"

"I honestly don't know. I don't think so," Dax said. "But the way it happened . . ."

"Get a grip on yourself, old man, and then tell me what you saw."

Dax swallowed and nodded. Apparently she, too, was thinking of the loss of the station, and what it meant to the entire sector. What it meant to our friends.

She took a deep breath. "The *Madison* simply exploded a photon torpedo in front of them, to warn them to stop. It didn't explode anywhere near the ships, but at that moment, every Mist ship exploded."

Every Mist ship. I stared at the debris floating around and through the ships in my usual reality. *Every Mist ship.*

"Could this have something to do with the differing molecular structures that you were talking about?" I asked Dr. Bashir.

"I don't think so," he said, not taking his gaze off the screen. "You see how the two kinds of matter interact. It's as if one can flow through the other."

"But a weapon—"

"A weapon should work the same way," Bashir said. "Otherwise you'd accidentally blow up ships in Mist space when you used a photon torpedo in ours."

Of course. Of course. This was beginning to make some sort of sense to me, but in a subconscious way. Over the years, I have learned to trust that feeling, to allow it, and not my conscious brain, to sort through things I did not entirely understand.

"Explain what happened again, old man," I said to Dax. "How did those ships explode?"

"It was as if someone pushed a button and they all just exploded."

"All at the same time?"

She nodded.

"Was it a chain reaction?"

"Oh, no," she said. "It happened too fast."

I felt cold. My subconscious brain did not like that.

I leaned forward in my captain's chair. I could not see anything on that screen but the exploded Mist ships overlaid on the Cardassian, Klingon, and alien ships.

"What about Captain Victor and the other home-world ships?" I was almost afraid of what her answer might be. If they were gone, we, too, were trapped in Mist space. Forever.

Her hands flew across her console. Apparently, in her concern and shock, Dax had not thought of our situation.

"They're fine," she said, and I felt a relief that I hadn't thought possible. "They're standing half a light-year off."

"I doubt it was the photon torpedo that caused this," I said. "Given what I understand of this, if it were the torpedo, the ships would have cascade-exploded in a chain reaction. They did not. So either there's a phenomenon we don't understand happening with our equipment or something else is going on."

And considering how difficult the situation had been with Captain Victor, how little he told us, and how often we found out the truth was slightly different, I would have wagered all of Quark's latinum that something else was going on. Perhaps the ships had had weapons, or, what I considered to be the more likely scenario, they had self-destructed when we took the first prisoners.

Prisoners. That brought me back to other matters. "Doctor, we have wounded in sickbay," I said.

"I know," he said. "I was just heading there when this happened." He gazed at the screen. "I would like to use the science station to see what caused this. If I get a chance, I'll run some tests in sickbay."

"Good," I said, doubting he would get that chance in the time we needed it.

He headed toward the turbolift. As he did so, I scanned the bridge. Dax had brought up replacement officers for my away team. They seemed as stunned as we were. The Vulcan transporter operator was here. Her name was T'Lak, and she was a competent engineer. O'Brien had hopes for her.

"Ensign T'Lak," I said, "take over the science station. See what you can determine."

My words reached her. She moved with military precision from her position near the turbolift to the science station. The security officer who stood in Worf's usual place, a young Bajoran man named Orla, met my gaze. In his eyes, I saw all the concern I felt for our own region of space. He knew as well as I did that we had to resolve this or Bajor was lost forever.

"Help her, Lieutenant Orla," I said.

He nodded, then bent over his console.

I didn't expect them to find anything—I don't even know if they knew what they were looking for—but I had to keep them busy while I thought this through.

I ran my hand over my scalp as if I still had hair to smooth. Dax looked at me, her eyes wide.

"None of this makes sense, old man."

"I know, Benjamin," she said. "I've been trying to think it through—"

"It makes sense to me," Cadet Nog said.

Dax and I both turned to him. He shrugged and gave us both a sheepish grin. He said, "My people believe there is profit to be made from both sides of a war. Sometimes playing one side against the other brings higher profits."

He was right, of course. It was an option I hadn't thought of because it was something that went against every inch of my being. I would have come to it eventually, but it would take time. That sort of betrayal—the kind that cost lives—was anathema to me.

"Thank you, Cadet," I said as I stood. "Dax, you have the bridge. I have some prisoners to talk to."

"Bah," Sotugh said. "You take advice from a Ferengi, and a Starfleet cadet at that."

Sisko smiled at Sotugh. "I take good ideas where I find them. And you must admit, he was right."

"Don't! Don't!" the Quilli said. "You're spoiling the story. Don't let that Klingon get you ahead of yourself."

Sotugh gave the Quilli a horrid threatening look. The Quilli's bristles rose and seemed to grow longer.

"I will close the bar," Cap said.

"Ah, Cap, it's a good old-fashioned stare-down," the Trill said. "Let them be."

But Sotugh broke the look. He waved a hand again.

"I do not waste my time with creatures one-tenth my size."

"And who have a hundred times your brainpower," the Quilli said.

Sotugh growled softly, but did not turn. Instead, he leveled his frown at Sisko.

"So tell them what you discovered from the prisoners," Sotugh said. "Just remember that while you were sitting, talking, I was fighting a pitched battle to save your station. Even though *they* do not want to hear of it."

"Does that matter?" Sisko asked. "You enjoyed every moment of that fight."

"True," Sotugh said, his frown suddenly changing to a laugh. "It *was* glorious."

The six prisoners filled the *Defiant*'s brig. They were an odd mix of humans, Bajorans, and Jibetians. They were all dirty and one seemed injured. She was lying on the cot, a hand over her face.

I stood facing the forcefield. "Who's in charge here?"

A human stood and moved to face me. He was squarely built. His dark eyes and rounded cheeks seemed more suited to laughter than to war.

"I am in charge," he said. "My name is John David Phelps Jackson."

I motioned for the guards to drop the forcefield for a moment, then indicated that Jackson should come with me. He glanced at his compatriots, as if in apology, then followed me to a small table where I sat and indicated that he do the same.

For a moment he looked as if he would remain standing, but I again indicated the chair. "Sit. We need to talk."

He did, making certain that his friends in the brig could still see his face.

"I'm afraid," I said, "that your ships have all been destroyed. What is left of your force on the station is in a very heated and, most likely, losing battle with Klingons."

"Destroyed?" Jackson said, his face going gray. "Why did you do that? They had no weapons."

"We did not," I said. "I can assure you of that. And neither did the Klingons. Your ships exploded all at the same moment. We have no explanation, yet."

Jackson leaned back in his chair and closed his eyes for a moment. When he sat back up there was a haunted look behind his eyes, as if he'd just seen a ghost and that ghost was going to kill him.

"What do you want from me, Captain Sisko?"

"I want to know what's going on. All I've been told is one side of this fight. Captain Victor and Councillor Näna's side. I would like to hear yours."

The frown of puzzlement that crossed Jackson's face made no sense to me at that moment. Then he leaned forward. "You have talked to Captain Victor?"

"Yes," I said.

"Then you know our side as well."

Now it was my turn to be confused. "He has told

me of your intentions with the station, and of your desire to be free from the homeworld rule, but—"

"Free of their rule?" Jackson said. "What are you talking about?"

I glanced at the people behind the forcefield, then back at Jackson. I sighed. It seemed, once again, that Captain Victor had been less than honest with me.

I leaned toward him and said, "I think it is time that I hear your side of exactly what is going on here."

CHAPTER
13

JACKSON LOOKED AT ME as if I were crazy. Remember, we had fought him and his compatriots, and then we had captured them, easily. Suddenly I was asking for his side. I must have seemed capricious and strange.

He glanced over his shoulder at his friends in the brig. Four of them were watching intently. The woman remained on her bunk.

"First," he said, "I need medical attention for Sasha. Then I'll talk to you."

I frowned at the two security officers. They did not meet my gaze. It was their duty to report any injuries among prisoners—injuries that were more serious, say, than a slight cut or bruise—and these officers hadn't done so. I knew that the anger at the capture of the station was running high, but it was not an excuse for dereliction of duty. Theirs would be noted in their files, and I would take care of the situation when this crisis was over.

I hit my comm badge. "Dr. Bashir," I said. "We have a patient needing treatment in the brig."

"I'm nearly finished here, sir," he said. "I'll send a member of my team down immediately."

"Good." Then I laid my hands flat on the table. "Your friend will be taken care of. Now, talk to me. We don't have much time."

Jackson studied me, eyes narrowing. "I don't see why I should tell you anything."

I had had enough. I was tired, I was worried, and I was under a very real deadline. "We both are facing a crisis," I said. "You have just lost all your ships. My station has been yanked into a part of space where it does not belong, causing a serious crisis in my space. We did not destroy your ships, and I have a hunch I know who did. Captain Victor told me you were his enemy, which leads me to believe you and I are both being used."

"I'm the *enemy?*" Jackson said, again sitting back and closing his eyes as he took in the information.

I decided the best course was to push. "Captain Victor said that you and the rest of the colonists were tired of Mist rule. He said that you had a plan to take the station and use it to control the Mist homeworld. He brought us and the Klingons into this space to stop you."

Jackson sat bolt upright, his eyes bright, his gaze focused on mine. "The rumors have been rampant for years that the Federation and Klingons intended to invade the Mist and use our technology. Captain

Victor's plan was to take over your station and use it as a defense against your attack."

My left hand clenched into a fist. I was angry, not just at Captain Victor, but at myself. All through this crisis, my gut had said things were not as they appeared. And although I noted the reaction, I did not act upon it.

"Until Captain Victor lured us into your space," I said, "we did not even know the Mist existed outside of the legends."

"You never intended to attack us?"

"Of course not," I said. "We usually don't attack without reason, and we never intentionally attack something we don't know exists."

Jackson stared at me for a moment, holding my gaze. There was power in those dark eyes. The man was a natural leader. "So, if you weren't going to invade us, none of this makes sense."

"Oh, it's making sense to me," I said, thinking of Nog's comment about profit. "But the only truth I know at the moment is that someone blew up your ships, and it was not us."

Then we heard the whine of a pneumatic door. Two medical technicians entered, and hurried to the brig. The barrier winked out, and they stepped inside. It immediately winked up again.

Jackson turned to me, his gaze level. I was keeping my promise; we both knew that. And I was not acting like a man bent on conquering a section of space.

He swallowed hard. "Is every one of my ships gone?"

I nodded.

He slapped a hand on the table and stood. The guards made a move toward him, but I signaled them to stay back. Thirty ships were gone; he had to have lost a lot of people. A lot of friends.

"All the ships near the station are gone," I said as gently as I could. "I assume those were yours. Including the two special ships."

"Special ships?" He turned and grabbed the back of his chair, looking down at me.

In his confusion, I knew the last of it, the last of it all. Captain Victor had lied to me about *everything*. I still did not understand his purpose in doing so, nor his point in bringing the *Defiant* over *before* the capture of the station, but I suspected it was all part of an elaborate ploy, a ploy that was beginning to unravel.

"Captain Victor told me that only two of your ships had the capability of bringing the station from the normal universe," I said. "He also told me that the station could only be returned by the same device."

Jackson half laughed. It was a desperate, bitter sound. "All our ships have the ability to bring something over from normal space. And any of them can return it if it hasn't been here too long."

"We did discover that problem on our own," I said. "If our calculations are correct, we may stay here a little over two hours. Right now, we have used up much of that time."

Jackson didn't seem to hear me. He appeared to be lost in his own thoughts. Slowly he sank back into his chair. "With the people thinking you destroyed all our ships, the war fever will reach an unstoppable level," he said. "Hundreds of Mist systems will declare war on your Federation, and the Klingon Empire."

"Hundreds?" The extent of the lies that I had been told—and that I had not had the time to check—was astounding me. Captain Victor was really an accomplished manipulator. His mixture of truth and falsehood was creative and plausible.

And worthless, now.

We were on the brink of a devastating war. Not only would we have the problems within our own space that I've already outlined—the defense of the wormhole, the problems with the Cardassians and the Klingons and, ultimately, the Dominion—but we would have to fight the Mist because *they* believed they were victims of an unprovoked attack. With their technology, they would defeat us in a matter of hours.

"I thought there were five systems," I said, my voice flat. I already knew that I was wrong.

"No," Jackson said. "There are two hundred and eight Mist systems in this quadrant."

"Ah, phooey," the Quilli said, and sat down, hard, in its chair. The Trill had to move his foot quickly before bristles stuck in his boot.

"Phooey?" Cap said, eyebrows raised.

"Yeah," the Quilli said. "Phooey. I thought this was a great story until now."

"You have an opinion, warthog?" Sotugh asked, sounding as offended as if he had been telling the story.

"Yeah," the Quilli said, "I do. I believe that there could be five Mist systems, but not two hundred and eight. First of all, where'd they get all the space? And secondly, if what Sisko said is true, they had to steal their population from our universe. Wouldn't *someone* have noticed?"

Sisko took a forkful of jambalaya, knowing now that the Quilli wouldn't care. The food was still hot, just as Cap predicted, and just as delicious.

"Sisko," Sotugh said. "It is your story."

Sisko swallowed, held up his hand so that he could get a moment, and then had a few gulps of ale. "I talked to Jackson about this later," he said. "The Mist learned how to shift out of normal time over two thousand years ago. There were five systems full of Mist at that time. Eventually, they expanded."

"But one new system every twenty years?" the Caxtonian said. "Come on."

Sisko wiped his mouth with his napkin and looked pointedly at the Quilli. "It was easy for them to find a system with no intelligent life and to bring it over," he said. "They needed the new systems for minerals, food, and manufacturing to supply the ever-expanding culture."

"But they had to have life-forms on those systems,"

the Quilli said. "You can't make me believe they had that kind of population explosion."

"I do not expect you to believe anything," Sisko said. "I'm telling you what Jackson told me."

"And he could've been lying like Captain Victor was."

Sisko smiled, thinking of John David Phelps Jackson. The man probably could lie, but would not do so unless he had to do so to save lives.

"He could have been," Sisko said, "but Jackson was not that kind of man. Remember, the Mist were constantly bringing in other races. The growth was solid and expanding. They also had no natural enemies. I later learned that there were over a million human Mist spread across twenty planets."

"And very few Klingons," Sotugh said.

"Fewer than a thousand," Sisko said. He looked at Sotugh and grinned. "And you know, they all have different facial features than you do."

"Bah," Sotugh said. "They left the Empire centuries ago. They are Klingon only by birth."

"Convinced now?" the Trill asked the Quilli.

The Quilli frowned, and its bristles moved forward. The frown was one of those expressions that made dangerous tiny creatures appear harmless and cute. Sisko was not fooled. "It is the first thing that has broken me out of the story's magic—naturally broken me out, not interrupted it," it said, looking at the others. Then it stood again, and bowed slightly to Sisko. "But in each story, the teller is allowed one impossible thing. I will give you this one. Do not have any more."

Cap put a fist to his mouth and turned away, hiding a grin. Sotugh rolled his eyes.

Sisko nodded solemnly. "I'll do my best," he said.

"Obviously," I said to Jackson, "Captain Victor and Councillor Nāna want to start a war between normal space and Mist space. We do not have time to discuss why. You and I need to call a truce between our forces. My people are running out of time."

Behind Jackson, the medical team helped the injured woman up. She was between them. They put their arms around her, and half carried her out of the brig. The remaining prisoners did not try to get away.

Jackson watched this, as I did, and then turned to me. "If you can return my belt," he said, "I can order a cease-fire."

I instructed the guard to do as Jackson asked, then release the others. I tapped my comm link. "Dax," I said. "Patch me through to Sotugh."

"Aye, Captain," she said.

One of the guards had left. The other still stood before the door. Jackson's people crowded near the barrier.

Then I heard Sotugh's voice over the comm link. "Go ahead, Sisko," he said.

"Cease hostilities," I said. "We have no fight with those on the station."

"Is this a trick, Sisko?" Sotugh said.

* * *

"If I had known you were doing this on the strength of one man's word," Sotugh said, "I would never have stopped the fighting."

Sisko had learned to take these interruptions as part of his story. He had taken, enjoyed, and swallowed a quick bite of jambalaya while Sotugh talked.

"Have you never taken a man on his honor before?" Sisko asked.

Sotugh scowled. "Human honor is a difficult concept, often debated among the Houses of the Empire."

"But it does exist," Sisko said.

"Sometimes," Sotugh conceded.

"This is not a trick," I said to Sotugh. "We have a much larger enemy and very little time to fight him. Meet me in Ops. We have a battle plan to discuss."

The guard had given Jackson his belt. He was using it to order a cease-fire.

There was a momentary pause, and then Sotugh said, "Bah, they have stopped fighting. There is no honor in killing men who do not fight. I will meet you."

I turned back to Jackson, who nodded to me. The worry lines on his face had eased slightly, and I realized he was a much younger man than I had initially thought. Young or not, he was clearly in control of his people.

"We need to figure out just what Captain Victor is up to," I said, "and then we need to stop him. But first, we are running out of time for my station. We must shift it back to real space. Do you know how we can do that?"

"With all of my ships destroyed," he said, "I don't think we can. Your station is going to be stuck in this space."

"Unacceptable," I said. "That is exactly what Captain Victor wants to happen, and we're not going to give it to him."

CHAPTER
14

"Bravo!" the Quilli said, clapping its tiny paws together.

"The story's not over, warthog," Sotugh said.

"It doesn't matter. I like tales of heroism and derring-do."

The Trill raised an eyebrow. "I take it that you have forgotten your disapproval."

"We may quibble about details," the Quilli said, "but quite frankly if the story's good, the details can be changed."

"You are going to sell this!" the Trill said.

"I never said that," the Quilli said, looking at Sisko, paws out as if it were shrugging its tiny shoulders. "I'm merely trying to help the captain here with his tale."

The Trill shook his head. "Don't trust a Quilli. Make sure it pays you something before it leaves. Believe me, it'll make a profit off you otherwise."

Sotugh's scowl grew. "The warthog seems to be fairly unpredictable. We will wait until Sisko is done before we will discover if this story meets the warthog's ideas of 'derring-do.'"

"You don't think it will?" Sisko asked him.

Sotugh shook his head. "The warthog is a little tiny creature covered with poisoned darts. Who knows what will please it?"

"It would please it to continue with the story," the Quilli said.

Cap actually laughed.

Sisko only smiled, and complied.

Jackson and I beamed into Ops to discover that the smoke had cleared, the fires were out, and my crew was hard at work repairing the station. Chief O'Brien was on his back near some fried paneling, his hands covered with soot as he worked.

Major Kira had not bothered to clean the dirt off her face or fix the sleeve of her uniform; she was sitting at her station, seeing what parts of *Deep Space Nine* were still on-line. From one of the comm links, I heard Security Chief Odo's voice growling about looters, but I could not tell to whom he was talking.

It did not matter. At this moment, we had to take care of the station.

As Jackson and I stepped off the transporter pad, Kira saw us. She raised a phaser so quickly that I did not see her hand move.

"Captain!" she said. "Stand aside. That's one of the men we were fighting."

"I know, Major," I said. "You can put your weapon down. Jackson and I have discovered a common cause."

Kira put down her phaser, but she narrowed her eyes in her "this had better be good" look.

I ignored it. "Major, I need a status report."

She sighed, knowing that I would not answer her unasked question immediately. She glanced at O'Brien. Except for a brief moment to observe the verbal altercation, he did not look away from his work.

"We'll have shields up in five minutes," she said. "Weapons are going to take another ten."

"She did a good job sabotaging the place," O'Brien muttered. He did not sound pleased.

"As she was ordered to do," I said. "Just put it back together as soon as you can. But the weapons are now our first priority."

"Captain, the shields—"

"I understand, Major," I said. "But the situation has changed. We need those weapons and we need them now."

"Yes, sir," Kira said.

O'Brien rolled away from the panel he was working on. Without bothering to close it, he moved to another, pulled it open, and started to work there.

At that moment Captain Higginbotham beamed onto the transporter pad. Higginbotham is a tall man who looks no different than he did when we were at the Academy together—except for the silver threading his dark wiry curls.

He wrinkled his nose at the stench of fried circuitry. "Remind me when I need a good saboteur to hire Major Kira," he said as he stepped off the pad.

"The situation has changed, Paul," I said.

"I gathered that when I saw the ships," he said. He nodded at Jackson, who did not nod back.

Then the turbolift clanged into place. The unusual sound made O'Brien lift his head from his work. Sotugh, his uniform covered with two phaser burns, stepped off.

"Four," Sotugh said. "Four phaser burns, Sisko. We were having a glorious pitched battle on the Promenade until you cut it off."

"Excuse me," Sisko said, not willing to quibble over details, although he was convinced he had only seen two phaser burns, "*four* phaser burns. No matter how you looked, we can agree on what you said."

"I said, 'Your explanation had better be a good one,'" Sotugh said.

"And I did not answer you immediately."

"No, you did not."

"Instead I turned to Major Kira."

"Are the sensors working?" I asked.

"Yes, sir," she said. "I didn't see any point in sabotaging those."

I moved over to a nearby panel and keyed in the main screen showing the scene outside. The Cardassians were still holding their positions near the wormhole but now there were at least a dozen Galor-class warships.

"A Klingon fleet of six will be here in less than thirty minutes," I said. "Three Federation starships will also be here by that point."

"It will be a glorious battle," Sotugh said.

"Yes," I said. "But it will be a fight staged by Captain Victor and the Mist. And I, for one, don't like fighting other people's battles."

"Staged?" Sotugh said.

I switched the screen to show the fleet of Mist ships now surrounding Captain Victor's ship half a light-year away. There were at least thirty, maybe more.

"Grey Squadron," Jackson said, staring at the screen with a look of shock. "I've never seen or heard of more than two in one place before."

"Grey Squadron?" Higginbotham asked.

Jackson half swallowed, then nodded without taking his gaze from the main screen. His eyes were touched with a hint of fear. "The Grey Squadron is made up of the only fully armed Mist ships. They've functioned as a sort of police force for centuries, keeping the peace among the hundreds of systems."

"Hundreds of systems?" Higginbotham asked, glancing sharply at me.

"Armed with what?" Sotugh demanded.

Jackson only shrugged. "No one really knows."

"Oh," I said, "Captain Victor knows. And our problem is that we must capture one of those ships within thirty minutes or we're not returning to normal space."

"What?" Major Kira said.

"Explain yourself," Sotugh demanded.

"Yes," Higginbotham said. "It seems there is a lot we haven't heard."

"I was beginning to think that I was the one who had been tricked," Sotugh said. "By you."

Sisko nodded. "I can understand that. You certainly were not set up to trust the Federation at that point in our histories. It is to your credit that you helped us and did not abandon everything at that point."

"I still think you are too gullible," Sotugh said, obviously pleased at Sisko's compliment.

"I think events were transpiring too fast to proceed on anything other than gut instinct," Sisko said.

"If I had done that, Sisko," Sotugh said, "I would have taken over your station myself."

Sisko shrugged and sipped his Jibetian ale. "That only proves my point, Sotugh. Events were transpiring too fast for us to do much more than stay ahead of them."

It took me a few short minutes to brief Captains Sotugh and Higginbotham, Major Kira, and Chief O'Brien.

"It seems that our focus," Higginbotham said, after I finished, "is to get a device under our control to shift us back to normal space. We shift the station first to get it out of here, and to forestall any problems in our space. Then we shift our ships back momentarily to buy more time."

"A good idea," Sotugh said.

"I think it's critical," I said, "that we don't let the station fall into Captain Victor's hands."

"And from the looks of those Cardassian ships," Major Kira said, "the station needs to be in normal space to stop a war."

I glanced at the screen. There were now more than a dozen Cardassian privateer ships near the wormhole and the number seemed to be growing by the minute. I turned to Jackson. "Do you have any other ships close by with the ability to shift?"

"Every starship has the shift device hooked to its warp drive," Jackson said. "But the closest ship would take an hour to get here, if it could get through the Grey Squadron."

"That's too long," I said.

"What about the debris?" Chief O'Brien asked Jackson.

"I don't understand," Jackson said, staring at the chief before glancing at me.

"Your ships," O'Brien said. "Is there any chance that one of the shift devices might have survived whatever blew them apart?"

Jackson glanced at the main screen, but none of the debris was visible. His entire face sagged. I knew that he saw not just debris, but the bodies of his crewmates. "One of them might have," he said after a moment. "They are well protected."

"Jackson, work with the chief to see what you can

find." I turned to Captain Higginbotham and Sotugh. "If we end up fighting the Mist ships, we need to remember that they can beam through our shields."

"And more than likely shoot through, also," Higginbotham said.

"Five against thirty," Sotugh said. "I would welcome such odds if we had shields. Without shields, there is only stupidity in such a death."

"So we need to find a way to shield against their weapons," I said.

"You know," Higginbotham said, stroking his chin and staring out the screen at the Grey Squadron, "if they have such an advantage, how come they aren't pouring in here to destroy us?"

"The way that Victor has set things up so far," I said, "has been to allow Jackson to do the fighting for him. I suspect he believes we are still fighting. It doesn't matter to him, as long as we remain here past our time limit. Then we will be trapped in the Mist's space."

"At which point they come in, call us invaders, and destroy us," Higginbotham said.

"I would imagine that is Captain Victor's plan."

"A coward's plan," Sotugh said.

"Captain," Chief O'Brien said. "We've found one shift device intact."

"Excellent, Chief. Beam over to the *Defiant* and get it hooked up."

"Captain," Jackson said, and three of us turned to him. He grinned for the first time since I met him, an infectious look. No wonder he was an effective leader.

"Captain Sisko," he corrected. "With our device hooked up, your ship will not be able to transfer your space. It will only be able to transfer other objects."

I glanced at Higginbotham and Sotugh.

"In fact," Jackson went on," anything that has been in Mist space too long will stop the shift."

Higginbotham gave me a concerned look. Sotugh shook his head, as if this obstacle was yet another personal affront.

"You must admit, the difficulties of this mission were increasing by the minute," Sotugh said. "I prefer quick, clean battles, with the sides carefully drawn."

"How Klingon of you," Prrghh said.

I did not like it either, but we had been lucky enough to find a device. We were going to use it.

"Chief," I said, "get busy. We need to get this station back where it belongs."

"Aye, sir," O'Brien said. He contacted Dax, and together they worked on a plan to get the device on board the *Defiant* while he beamed over.

"Gentlemen," I said to Captains Sotugh and Higginbotham, "I need your crews to work on a solution to the problem of the shields. Captain Victor beamed onto the *Defiant*. I'm sure we have information about the effect that beam-in had on our equipment. I'll have Dax transfer that to your ships. It will give your people a place to start."

"You still see a coming fight with Captain Victor, don't you?" Higginbotham asked.

I nodded. "Even if we retreat back into normal space, he's going to tell everyone that we destroyed the ships in an aborted invasion into Mist space."

"Why would he do that?" Higginbotham asked. "I have been trying to figure this out and it makes no sense."

"I have been wondering the same thing," I said. I glanced at Jackson. He was working with Kira and not monitoring our conversation. "Greed, perhaps? Control? Some kind of power transfer? I plan to ask Captain Victor the next time I see him."

"Right before you kill him, if I have not done so first," Sotugh said.

Higginbotham opened his mouth, probably to tell Sotugh that that is not the Federation way, when I caught his eye and shook my head. Higginbotham said nothing.

"Which was a good thing," Sotugh said. "The last thing I would have wanted to know was that I was fighting alongside men without honor."

"We have honor," Sisko said. "It's just different from yours."

Sotugh looked at the other patrons. "And now you see why we Klingons debate the nature of human honor. It is as slippery and changeable as a Belopian eel."

Sisko grinned. "I ignored the question of killing Captain Victor, and instead said . . ."

* * *

"If we don't get him stopped now, the Mist will declare war on the Federation and Empire and that will be the end of both our cultures."

Higginbotham nodded. The full impact of what we were facing was slowly dawning on him. "They can transfer one ship at a time into their space and destroy it."

"Or one person at a time," I said.

"There is no honor in fighting an unseen enemy," Sotugh said.

"Then we fight them now, while we can see them," I said. "We need shields, gentlemen. And we need them quickly. Get your crews working on the solution. Then we will come up with a battle plan."

"The sooner the better," Higginbotham said.

"If we do this right, the battle will be glorious," Sotugh said.

"Maybe," I said. "If that shift device works and we can modify the shields to stop Mist fire."

"Details," Sotugh said, waving his hand and looking more confident than he had since he arrived in Ops. "Those are nothing but petty details."

CHAPTER
15

"PETTY DETAILS?" Prrghh said, standing up and stretching, arching her back slightly and touching the tip of her small tongue to her upper lip. Her back was impossibly flexible. She straightened and looked at Sotugh. "Trust a Klingon to be overconfident."

"We were not overconfident," Sotugh said. "I knew it was going to be a glorious battle."

"Seems to me it either had to be glorious or you were all dead." The Trill got up and went to the bar. He ordered Canar, which made everyone look at him as if he were crazy.

Everyone except Cap, that is. He turned around, took a bottle of Canar off the shelf, and asked the Trill if he wanted a glass or the entire bottle.

"The entire bottle, of course," the Trill said. "If it's good Canar."

"You drink that Cardassian garbage?" Sotugh asked.

The Trill shrugged. "Just because you disagree with a race's political habits doesn't mean you should ignore the things they do well. I usually go for a good blood wine, but tonight, during this story, I prefer Canar."

Tonight? Sisko frowned. He wondered how long he had been in here. Sometimes it felt like days; sometimes it felt like minutes. He'd been here long enough to ruin a plate of nachos and to have Cap's cook make jambalaya from scratch. Several hours at least.

"I'm a little confused," the wraith said. It moved away from the wall, looking almost like an opaque shadow in motion. "Can I see if I have the facts straight?"

"Shoot," Sisko said, picking up his fork. He might be able to finish this jambalaya after all. He took a bite. Wonderfully, the jambalaya was *still* warm. What kind of bowl did Cap use? Did it have its own heating source?

"Okay." The wraith folded itself on top of a table, looking like a bit of wax that was bending itself into a vaguely human shape. "This is how I understand it. In normal space, you have a possible battle between a Cardassian fleet and a Klingon fleet over control of the wormhole. Correct?"

"And the Federation," Sisko said, around a mouthful of jambalaya. His words were nearly unintelligible.

Sotugh seemed to notice and added, "Three starships would arrive on the scene at the same time as the Klingons."

The wraith stretched a thumb. It extended and thinned like a piece of taffy. Only when the wraith let go of it, it snapped back into position with a loud *thwap!* "And the only thing that might stop the fight is the return of *Deep Space Nine* to normal space?"

"That is what we believed," Sisko said, being as cagey as he could. He didn't want to spoil the story, not after he had put this much time into it.

"We thought," Sotugh said, "that with the station and its firepower there, the Cardassians might not try to control the wormhole, or risk a war with the Federation."

"Seems unlikely to me," the Caxtonian said, his fetid breath filling the bar. Sisko's eyes watered, and he had to put his fork down. "But then I've always believed that the Cardassians let that station go too easily."

Sotugh shot him a withering glance. The Caxtonian didn't even seem to notice.

Neither did the wraith. It stretched a forefinger. "Then in Mist space," it said, letting the finger *thwap!* into place. Sisko suddenly realized this must be its equivalent of the human gesture of raising fingers to count. "The *Defiant*, Sotugh's three battle cruisers, and the *Starship Madison* are facing a fleet of Mist ships. And you don't have shields that are effective against them."

"Exactly," Sisko said.

The wraith took its middle finger. As it started to extend it, the Trill at the bar took a step over and grabbed the wraith's hand. The Trill looked a little green.

"You're putting me off my Canar," the Trill said softly.

"Oh!" The wraith glanced at him. "Sorry." It reached for its finger again, then—literally—balled up its hand and let it absorb into its waxlike body.

"If you were to keep the station," it said, "you would stand a chance against the Mist fleet, but you must send the station back to keep it from getting stuck in Mist space."

"And stop the fight between the Cardassians and Klingons," Prrghh said. "It's really not that complicated a story. You're making it harder than it is."

"I just want to be clear," the wraith said.

"Don't you find this to be another impossible situation?" the middle-aged woman at the bar asked the Quilli.

"No," it said. "I find it fascinating, and I would like to hear more. But I have decided to have patience. I believe that these interruptions must be a human way of storytelling."

"It's the way stories are told in bars," the middle-aged man said.

Cap grinned at him. "You sound like an authority."

The man shrugged, then put an arm around the middle-aged woman. The casualness of the gesture told Sisko that either these two had been together a long time, or they were married or both. "After seventeen years of bartending," the man said, "you get to be an expert on just about anything that happens in a bar."

"A Quilli telling a story in a bar would never allow this many interruptions," the Quilli said.

"A Quilli telling a story in *this* bar wouldn't have a choice," the Trill said. He took his bottle of Canar and returned to his table. "So, our finger-snapping buddy over here is pretty clear on the concept and since no one else is asking questions, I assume everyone else is. You could probably continue."

"Good," Arthur said from behind the bar. "Because I've been wondering what plan you and Captain Sotugh and Captain Higginbotham come up with to solve this and keep the Mist from attacking normal space."

"If you'd let him finish his story," the Caxtonian said, "we'd all know."

Sisko reluctantly pushed the jambalaya away. "Well," he said, settling back into the story. . . .

It took us less than five minutes to work out a plan of attack—

"Ah, geez, you aren't going to tell us the plan, are you?" Arthur said.

"Shh," the Quilli said. "It's a storytelling ploy, and a good one for building suspense. Go on, Captain."

Captains Sotugh and Higginbotham had beamed back to their ships. I went to help Major Kira while

Odo, my chief of security, made certain that all of Jackson's personnel and equipment were on board the *Defiant*.

Despite what Kira had said earlier, she and Chief O'Brien had done a great deal of work on the weapons. It only took the two of us two and a half minutes to get the weapons on-line. It took another two and a half minutes to get them powered to eighty percent. It took us another two minutes to get the screens back on-line. That left exactly fourteen minutes to shift the station or have it forever trapped in Mist space.

I used the station's communications to contact the *Defiant*. "Chief," I said without preamble. "We're running out of time."

"This is one strange machine," O'Brien said. "I haven't had much time to study it, but I think we've got it working." He paused for a moment, then added. "Dax tells me she's found another intact shifter in the debris."

"Good," I said. "Tell her to get it on board. If she finds any more, have her beam them on as well. Let's take as many precautions as we can while remembering our time constraints."

"Will do," O'Brien said.

"After she beams that on, stand by," I said.

"Aye, sir."

I closed the communication with the *Defiant* and immediately contacted the *Madison*. Higginbotham appeared on our screens. He was doing hands-on work. I could tell from the smudge of grease along his left cheek.

"Well, Paul?" I asked. "How are the shield modifications coming?"

"To be honest, Ben," Higginbotham said, "I have no idea if what we've done will work. My engineer and my science officer have differing opinions. My engineer is uncertain, but Dr. Jones is adamant. She says it will work."

I'd met Jones. She was one of the sharper minds in Starfleet. "Let's hope that Dr. Jones is correct," I said, "because we are out of time and options. I'm going to shift the station, the *Madison,* and the Klingon ships back to real space in exactly four minutes."

"Got it," Higginbotham said. "Good luck."

His image disappeared from our screen.

I turned to Major Kira. "Get those shield modifications from the *Madison* in case I have to bring you back to Mist space. When we shift the station back over to normal space, it will be up to you to deal with the Cardassians."

She smiled. Her teeth were very white against her filthy, battle-worn skin. "Oh, that will be my pleasure," she said.

"Major," I said, both enjoying and worrying about her enthusiasm, "deal with them peacefully, if possible."

"You take all the fun out of it," she said, her grin widening. I knew that she would do her best, and that she would stay within the parameters set by Starfleet. I also knew that this situation could get out of hand, quickly.

"As soon as I reach the *Defiant,*" I said, heading to the transporter pad, "be prepared to shift to our home space. But remember, we may need your help here if things start going sour. So be ready."

"Understood," she said. "Good luck."

That was the second time someone had wished me good luck in the space of five minutes. Such a wish usually meant that the speaker had no faith in the procedure ahead. I knew that we were operating on a by-gosh and by-golly basis. Our chances for success depended on a series of happy coincidences and on the ability of our engineers—mine and Captain Higginbotham's—to analyze and compensate for unfamiliar equipment, and then make it work the first time.

I had faith in Chief O'Brien and I knew that Higginbotham's new engineer, Braun Ginn, was one of the best in the fleet. But sometimes we asked too much of these talented people.

Apparently Higginbotham and Kira both thought this was one of those times.

"You mean," said a man at the bar who hadn't spoken until now, "that you've gone through situations before where a plan like this would work?"

He sounded completely skeptical. Sisko had been watching him during the story. The man was large, with a full white head of hair and matching beard. He smoked a meerschaum pipe that made him look as if he belonged in the nineteenth century instead of the twenty-fourth. Even his clothing had that old-fashioned sense.

Sisko smiled. "The history of Starfleet is filled with engineers who have made things work on a whim and a prayer," he said. "Beginning with Zefram Cochrane."

"You could make the argument," said the middle-aged man at the bar, "that the history of human spaceflight is filled with engineers like that. Think of the Mir space station in the twentieth century. That thing was up there for at least a decade longer than it should have been and I swear by the time they retired it, it was held together by spit and glue."

"Humans have always been that way," the woman beside him said. "Think of the Wright brothers."

"Columbus," the Trill said.

"I've always thought of him as an incompetent," the white-bearded man said. "Imagine sailing one way and believing you were sailing another."

"Robinson," Cap said, "we'll have time for your opinions later."

"You let Bo'Tex express his," Robinson said.

"Yes," Cap said, "but I didn't warn him two days ago about antagonizing the other patrons, like I had to warn you."

"Nope," Robinson said. "You just reminded him to bathe!"

At that moment, Sisko realized they were talking about the Caxtonian. No wonder the place didn't smell completely like Caxtonian body odor. Cap kept his customers in line.

"Someday," Sisko said, "I will tell you stories about the great engineers of the post-warp era, starting with Cochrane, going through Ty'lep and Montgomery Scott, and ending with a few that I know personally, like Miles O'Brien."

"I'd like to hear it," Robinson said, obviously mollified.

"Maybe next," the Quilli said, clapping its tiny paws together.

"What, do you have a quota or something?" the Trill asked. "You've been asking for a lot of stories."

The Quilli shrugged. "Maybe I like stories better than I like"—it grimaced at the bottle of Canar—"liquor."

"Or maybe you see a way to make a small fortune off this place," the Trill said. "Hey, Cap. Is it legal for a Quilli to be here?"

"If it's a captain, it is," Cap said. "I don't ban patrons from this place just because they act according to their culture's precepts."

The Trill narrowed his gaze, and then grinned. "Touché," he said. "Hadn't thought of it that way. So this is a sort of 'storyteller beware' place."

"Every place is," Cap said. "Some just aren't as obvious as others."

"Does it bother you to have the Quilli listening?" the middle-aged woman asked Sisko.

Sisko smiled at the small creature. "It's a good audience," he said.

"Thank you," the Quilli said, making a small

formal bow. "And I am finally getting used to these interruptions. Although I would like to know if you got the station back to its own space."

"Yes," the Trill said dryly. "I think we're all ready for a fight."

Sisko didn't know if the Trill meant inside the bar or inside the story, and he didn't really care. He pushed the nearly empty bowl of jambalaya aside and went back to the tale.

After the destruction I had been dealing with on the station, it felt good to be back on the *Defiant,* where things appeared to be running smoothly. Worf had returned to his security post. Dax was still at the helm. Cadet Nog looked like he belonged on communications.

Dax had the Grey Squadron on the screen. Individually, those ships had been beautiful. En masse, they looked like a fleet of ancient warships about to attack a defenseless village.

I dropped into the command chair and contacted Chief O'Brien in engineering. "Chief," I said. "Are you ready?"

"As ready as I'll ever be," the chief said. "This will work like a charm. I've got the shifter attached to the warp coil and the controls hooked up on the tractor beam. Jackson and two of his people are right here to help me."

That eased my worry a bit. Jackson, at least, should have known how this shifter worked.

* * *

"Your faith in an unknown human astounds me," Sotugh muttered.

"I've noticed that humans are an incredibly optimistic species," the Trill said.

"That's a charitable way of putting it," Prrghh said, as she crossed her arms and leaned back in the chair.

I asked the chief, "How about the shields?"

"I've made the shield modifications that the chief engineer of the *Madison* suggested," O'Brien said. I could almost hear him shrug. When he spoke like that, his attitude was that the idea might work, but he wasn't going to stake anything important on it. I never knew how to take that attitude. O'Brien usually didn't trust any engineer's work but his own—unless, of course, he had trained that engineer from the ground up.

"Good," I said to him. "Stand by."

"Standing," he said.

I grinned. We were always at our best at moments like this.

"Dax," I said. "Are all of Jackson's personnel aboard?"

"People and equipment," Dax said.

"Cadet, open a secure channel to both the *Madison* and the *Daqchov*," I said.

"Yes, sir," Nog said.

A moment later the main screen split. Sotugh was

on one, still looking battle-scarred with his four phaser burns—

"Finally got it right," Sotugh said.

—and Higginbotham was on the other, wearing just a bit more grease. After working to repair the station, I must have looked in the same sort of state.

"We're ready," I said. "We will shift the station first. Then we will shift your ships, Sotugh, and then the *Madison.*"

"Get us back quickly," Higginbotham said. "The Mist fleet is going to be on you in no time."

"Oh," I said, "I have no desire to fight them alone."

"Good," Sotugh said. "No point in taking all the glory."

I indicated that Nog should cut the communication.

"Chief," I said. "Ready?"

"Ready, sir," he said from engineering.

"Okay, old man," I said to Dax. "Put the station back where it belongs."

CHAPTER
16

DAX BENT OVER her console. Her fingers moved with great confidence, but she was biting her lower lip again.

"I'm turning on the beam," she said, "and pointing it at the station."

I gripped my chair.

Worf raised his head to watch.

Nog sat down for the first time during this mission.

Dax continued to work.

On the main screen, a line of white mist seemed to form in space, expanding like a cloud and flowing over the station, making it look slightly hazy. It seemed as if we were at sea, and the station were being covered by a great fog. The normally clear outline of the station became indistinct; then it blurred.

And then, suddenly, clarity returned.

The white mist disappeared. From our vantage, it looked like the station had passed through a very thin cloud and emerged on the other side, completely unchanged.

I could see nothing different. The station hung in its normal place. The Cardassian ships hovered near the wormhole, and a half-dozen Klingon ships were dropping out of warp.

"It didn't materialize on anyone?" Prrghh asked with great disappointment. She had a bloodthirsty look in her eyes that Sisko had suspected was there but hadn't seen until now. "I've been waiting this entire story to see what would happen when the station reappeared in the spot where someone else was."

"I thought I had been clear about that," Sisko said. He took a sip of Jibetian ale. "I had said that the station looked the same, with the ships around it, even though it was phased into Mist space."

"Yeah?" Prrghh said. "So?"

"So no one had moved into the space that the station had previously occupied," Sisko said.

"No one?" Prrghh asked.

"No one," Sisko said.

Prrghh shook her head, and leaned her chair back on two legs. She looked over her shoulder at the Quilli. "There's another impossible thing for you," she said. "I'd say the story's worthless."

"Nonsense," the Quilli said. "You just don't pay attention."

"I do," Prrghh said. "But with all those ships, one of them would have moved into the station's space."

The Quilli patted down its bristles as if it were wearing a suit and searching its vest pockets for something. The habit appeared to be a nervous one.

"Forgive me for being so bold," the Quilli said.

"As if you were not bold before," Sotugh growled.

"But what Sisko said about the station makes perfect sense to me. In fact, it seems illogical for someone to move into the station's spot," the Quilli said.

"It doesn't seem illogical to me," Prrghh said.

"It would if you were there," the Quilli said. "Imagine going to a space station you always go to. Then it disappears. Vanishes, right before your eyes. Would you fly your ship in those coordinates? Especially right after the thing vanished?"

Everyone in the bar turned to Prrghh. It was a captaining question, a leadership question. Would you take your precious ship with its valuable cargo and its even more valuable crew, and risk it on an insignificant shortcut through a bit of space occupied by something as large as a Cardassian-built space station a moment before?

Prrghh seemed to struggle with the question, not, Sisko believed, because she would make such a grievous mistake, but because she didn't want to lose face. She set her chair back down on all four legs.

"Well," she said, "when you put it that way, no. I wouldn't."

"See?" the Quilli said. "Not impossible at all."

"Well," the Trill said. "One war's been averted. Let's see if Sisko averted another one."

Sisko smiled. "After the white mist vanished, Dax said . . ."

"Transfer complete."

I couldn't tell the difference. I squinted at the screen. "Are you certain?"

Dax checked her instruments. Behind me, I heard corresponding beeps as Worf checked his.

"I'm positive, Captain," she said.

"Then let's get Sotugh's ships transferred. Quickly." I hit my comm badge. "Jackson, I need you on the bridge at once."

"All right, Sisko," Jackson said. He was making a point of not calling me by my title. It was, I think, his way of regaining some personal power after being held prisoner.

"I'm turning on the beam," Dax said, "and aiming at the Klingon ships."

She rarely used so many words to describe a procedure, but we had no shorthand for this one. I turned to the screen just in time to see another white line of mist form, expand into a small cloud, and flow over the Klingon ships. They, too, became indistinct, almost ghostly forms of their selves, and then they became solid again.

The white mist disappeared.

I remember thinking, *What an odd device,* and also *This must be how people without transporters regard our technology.*

"Transfer complete," Dax said. She was shaking

her head slightly as if she couldn't believe what she was seeing either.

Cadet Nog swiveled his chair toward me. "Major Kira is hailing the Cardassians," he said.

I had to take care of one problem at a time. "Dax, transfer the *Madison* to normal space."

"Beginning transfer," she said, finally developing a way of describing what she was doing.

The white mist formed, and engulfed the *Madison*. The starship seemed small and insignificant in the mist. I wondered if that was because the white mist mimicked a natural phenomenon on my home planet, Earth. No matter how far we go into the stars, the natural phenomena of our homes always seem more powerful than we are.

The *Madison*'s clean lines became blurry. Then the mist evaporated, and the *Madison* looked like herself again.

"Transfer complete," Dax said for a third time.

"Captain." Nog sounded panicked. "Captain Victor is demanding that he speak with you. Captain Sotugh is talking to the Klingon ships, and the *Madison* has contacted the other Starfleet vessels. Major Kira is still hailing the Cardassians."

"It sounds like the Tower of Babel out there, doesn't it, Cadet?" Dax asked with a grin.

"Huh?" Nog said, clearly not understanding the reference.

* * *

"I don't either," said the Quilli.

Several other alien voices chimed in as well.

"It's an Earth reference," the Trill said. "From one of their religious documents."

"How do Trills know about it?" the wraith asked.

The Trill smiled. "Trills make a point of knowing every good reference in the quadrant," he said.

Behind me, I heard the doors to the turbolift open. I spun my chair in time to see Jackson stride across the bridge. He seemed calm and self-assured. It was a nice contrast to the cadet's burgeoning panic.

"Everything has shifted back," I said to Jackson. "Are you ready?"

"I hope this works," he said, and I heard worry in his voice. Already he had mastered one of the main elements of command. No matter how concerned you are, always seem calm. If he lived through this, he would be a fine commander someday.

"That does not work with Klingons," Sotugh said, as he stood to get more blood wine.

"All we need is a little time," I said to Jackson. Then I stood and gave Jackson my command chair. He looked at it as if sitting in it would be a violation of some unwritten rule. Instead, he stood in front of it, much as I did when I spoke to others on screen.

"Dax," I said. "Make certain that the focus is on Jackson only. Everyone else remain quiet. Nog, I want this conversation to go out on a very wide band."

"Understood," Dax said.

"Yes, sir," Nog said.

"Connect him with Captain Victor," I said.

I moved over and stood near Nog, monitoring the young cadet. So far, he had acquitted himself well, but he did not dare make a mistake now. And as we all know, monitoring such wide and varied communications, while handling important ones of your own, can make for some interesting—and deadly—mistakes.

As it turned out, I needn't have worried. Nog handled the situation just fine. But at the time, I monitored everything.

Captain Victor appeared on screen. He was wearing his yachting cap low over his forehead, nearly obscuring his dark eyes. He did not look happy. Councillor Näna, beside him, seemed the same as ever. Näna's round mouth opened and closed for apparently no reason. His left eye wandered, and his right one was obscured by the screen.

Jackson put his hands on his hips and grinned. It was a powerful, cocky look, one that not many men could have carried off. Jackson made it look normal.

"Captain Victor," Jackson said. "Councillor."

"Jackson!" Victor sounded panicked. "What happened?"

"We captured this ship," Jackson said, "along with the station. However, it was clear that the Federation and Klingons had nothing to do with the destruction of our ships, and have no ability to shift into our space. They were brought over against their will, so we sent them back."

"You sent them *back?!*" Victor took a step closer to the screen as if he wanted to come through it and strangle Jackson himself. "You were not authorized to do that!"

Jackson let his grin slip. His expression hardened. It was clear just how dangerous this man could be. "I didn't realize I had to be authorized to take appropriate action."

"Jackson, your action was not appropriate," Victor said, obviously trying to get control of himself. "You don't understand what you have done!"

"Oh, I think I do," Jackson said. "Your information was incorrect about the Federation invasion. Up until you brought one of their ships over, and tricked my crews into bringing over their station, they didn't know we existed."

Captain Victor stiffened up like a statue. Beside him, Councillor Näna's mouth closed, and remained closed.

"How dare you accuse me of such things?" Victor said.

"I don't dare anything, Victor," Jackson said. His expression was now so hard that he looked nothing like the man who had grinned at Victor a moment before. "I have proof that you and your Grey Squadron blew up my ships. My planet's representative to the High Council will not be happy when he learns of your ploy. The entire High Council will not be happy."

For a moment Captain Victor seemed to hold his breath as his face reddened. Then slowly his eyes grew cold and his face seemed to change. "The High Council," he said, as if he were speaking of an annoying child. "The High Council is no longer important. We will simply destroy you, bring the station back over, and rule the Mist with it."

"An excellent plan," Jackson said, letting his arms drop. "In fact, an elegant plan, given its simplicity. It probably would work too, if the Grey Squadron were with you."

"They're with me, Jackson," Victor said. "They've always been with me." He moved closer to the screen. "And you have just guaranteed your death."

Then the screen went blank.

"Excellent," the wraith said. "You were broadcasting to the entire Mist. They saw Captain Victor for what he was, to stop them from thinking the Federation had attacked."

"That was my hope," Sisko said, nodding. Then he went on with the story.

"The Greys are moving," Dax said.

"Put it on screen," I said. "Let's keep a close eye on them, while we get the Federation and the Klingon ships back here."

"Aye, sir," Dax said. She bent over her console, performing the unfamiliar procedure.

"Transferring now," she said.

A white mistlike strip formed in space near the *Madison,* expanded to a cloud, and swept over it. Then the same thing repeated over the other two Federation starships. As I watched, the same cloud swept over the *Daqchov* and the other eight ships of the Klingon fleet.

I left communications in the cadet's capable hands, and walked over to Jackson. He grinned at me. "I think I could get used to commanding one of these."

"You'd have to go through Starfleet Academy first," I said, grinning back. "Although I must say, you might want to join the Mist version of the Royal Shakespeare Company. That was a hell of a performance."

"Very convincing," Nog said without looking up from the communications array.

"I think you bought enough time for the ships to adjust their shields," I said. "Good work."

"I hope so," Jackson said. "With that man ruling the Mist, nothing in this quadrant will be safe. In either space. That much has become very clear."

"Captain," Dax said. "In one minute, the Greys will be in range."

"Messages are coming in from the *Daqchov* and the *Madison,*" Nog said. "They're ready."

"Good," I said. "Open a hailing channel to Captain Victor. Again make sure this is broadcast as far as possible."

"Yes, sir," Nog said.

Both Jackson and I turned to face the screen as Captain Victor's face appeared. Until that day, I had never seen a human being's face turn purple with rage. But Captain Victor's did. He sputtered a moment before getting a word out.

"A Federation trick," Captain Victor said. "I thought so."

Councillor Näna had moved far away from him. Näna's mouth remained closed, and it appeared that his left eye had rolled inside his gray head.

"It was no trick," I said. "Jackson told the truth. And he's asked us and the Klingons to help him stop you from taking control. We have agreed."

"That is the truth," Jackson said. "You will not disband or destroy the council."

"I thought you didn't interfere in the internal affairs of others," Victor said to me.

I almost laughed. But I was conscious of our audience. "You brought us into this, Victor. You are responsible for our presence. You must live with the consequences."

"No," Victor said. "You must. You think a few weak Starfleet ships and some broken-down Klingon cruisers can stop the Grey Squadron?"

Jackson smiled. "Oh, I think so. And for the sake of the council and all the Mist worlds, I hope so."

"Be prepared to die," Victor said, and severed the communications. After a moment of darkness, the screen went back to showing the Grey Squadron. The ships looked even more menacing than they had before. They were well named.

"They'll be here in thirty seconds," Dax said.

"We have another problem, Captain," Worf said.

"I knew this resolution was too easy," the Quilli said, rubbing its paws together with glee.

"It's the Cardassians," Worf said. "They have taken up attack formation around the station."

I looked at the scene before me. Beyond the Grey Squadron, the station floated in its normal space. The Cardassians had formed an attack squadron around it. Suddenly we had a two-front battle, and to be honest, I wasn't sure we could win either of them.

CHAPTER
17

"DID YOU FORGET ABOUT your own ship?" the wraith asked, pulling on its fifth finger. The finger stretched and stretched, looking like a thin piece of gum.

The Trill was out of his seat, heading toward the wraith, as the wraith let go. The *thwap* echoed throughout the bar.

Several patrons—not just the Trill—shuddered.

Sisko found the whole finger thing kind of fascinating, but he was glad he was no longer eating.

The Trill grabbed the wraith's hand and squeezed it until it formed a doughlike impression of the Trill's fist. "Don't do that again," the Trill said. "It's disgusting."

"My people find it rather sexy," the wraith said.

The Trill made a face, and wiped his hands vigorously on his pants. Sisko got the sense that the wraith was grinning.

The wraith's hand re-formed into a normal,

human-shaped hand. "Well?" he asked. "Did you forget?"

"No, I hadn't forgotten," Sisko said. "I simply hadn't had time to remind my crew of the problem. Besides, we could not do anything until the *Madison* or the *Daqchov* were back in Mist space. And when that happened, our hands were suddenly quite full."

"Oh, no," Prrghh said. "Don't tell me you lost your ship."

Several patrons groaned.

"Sisko strikes me as the sort of man who would go down with his ship," Robinson said. "I suspect the *Defiant* was fine."

"I think we're getting a little ahead of the story here," the Quilli said, sounding more like Sisko's first-year intergalactic literature instructor at the Academy than Sisko would like to think about.

"We have a two-front battle going on, and all you people can do is chatter. Have you no discipline?" Sotugh asked.

So the end of the story interested him, despite everything. Sisko suppressed a grin.

"We have discipline, just not when we're drinking," the middle-aged man said.

"I'm sorry," the wraith said. "It's just that I was curious—"

"It was a good question," Sisko said, "and one I needed to deal with because time was running out. However, I had the Grey Squadron and the Cardassians to worry about at that moment."

"Couldn't you have let the station take care of the

Cardassians?" the Quilli asked, then clapped a paw over its mouth. The entire bar burst into laughter. The Quilli had learned some bad habits in the Captain's Table.

"If you do that on Quilla," the Trill said, "you lose your license to tell stories."

"I was just getting into the spirit of things," the Quilli said through its paw.

"To answer your question," Sisko said, "no, I could not. Even though I captained the *Defiant,* my true command was—and is—of *Deep Space Nine.* If I lost her to the Cardassians, the results would have been disastrous."

"I never did understand why the privateers attacked. Did they know of the Cardassian-Dominion alliance that soon?" Sotugh asked.

"No," Sisko said. "I have not understood it either, but my best guess is one that Dr. Bashir put forward after we recaptured the station."

"And the theory was?" Sotugh asked.

"They were acting like all pirates, looking for profit. They were planning to hold the wormhole for ransom."

"The Grey Squadron!" someone yelled from the back. Surprisingly, several patrons turned as if the fleet were coming through the door.

Sisko grinned. "Sorry," he said, and spun his empty Jibetian ale bottle with his fingers. Cap took it from him, and went back to the bar, probably to get him a new one.

"I told Dax," Sisko said, "to put us in the middle of

the Federation and Klingon ships. That way, if it looked like any of them were getting into trouble—"

"You could shift them back to normal space, out of trouble!" the wraith said.

"Exactly," Sisko said.

Dax instantly implemented my order. Then I turned to the cadet.

"Nog," I said. "I want you to monitor the situation between the Cardassians and the station. If the Cardassians attack, I want to know at once."

"Yes, sir," Nog said.

"Second, Cadet," I said, "I want this battle broadcast on an open band. I want all the Mist worlds seeing what is happening here."

Nog nodded, and bent over his panel. After watching him work a few moments before, I had a great deal more confidence in his abilities. The cadet would be an excellent officer one day.

"Bah!" Sotugh said. "Such confidence in a Ferengi."

Then I turned to Commander Worf. He was glowering at the situation in front of him. "Mr. Worf," I said. "Put our shields up and have our weapons ready."

"Aye, sir," Worf said.

On the main screen the nine Klingon ships had spread out on the left, taking up an attack formation facing the approaching Mist fleet.

On the right, the *Starships Madison, Idaho,* and *Cochrane* were in position, forming a wedge. Dax had placed the *Defiant* in the middle, and slightly behind the rest, giving us a complete view of the coming battle.

The Grey Squadron of the Mist was a both intimidating and beautiful sight. Their swept-back wing configuration made them look more like a flock of birds fanning out through the blackness of space. They were no more than half the size of most of the ships they were facing. Even the *Defiant* was larger than the largest Mist ship. Yet they outnumbered us by almost two to one.

And I had no idea if our shields would hold against their weapons.

We were going to either give them a fight, or get torn from space. At that moment I had no idea which it was going to be.

"If I had any idea you were such a pessimist, Sisko, I would never have agreed to fight with you," Sotugh said. "I knew we would overcome the Mist."

Sisko smiled and took a new Jibetian ale from Cap. "My people believe overconfidence is dangerous," he said.

"My people believe that unrealistic pessimism is grounds for demotion," Sotugh said.

"Sounds like you were ready to face anything that was going to come at you," the Trill said. He was not being sarcastic.

"I like to think we were," Sotugh said. "Obviously Sisko did not."

"I had a lot to think about then," Sisko said. "At that moment, Dax told me the Grey Squadron had come into range."

The squadron formed a line in front of us, like thirty ravens, bent on destruction.

"Let them fire the first shot," I said, more to myself than to anyone else.

For a moment I honestly didn't think anyone was going to fire. Then Captain Victor's ship fired a bright blue beam, hitting the *Defiant* and rocking us slightly.

Our shields held.

I wanted to cheer, but didn't.

A second later, space was full of bright blue beams, cutting through the blackness like flashlights cutting the dark as all the Grey Squadron opened fire on us.

The Mist ships scattered and attacked randomly as they swept in on the Klingons and Federation ships.

The *Defiant* was caught with two blasts, rocking us so hard that Jackson was tossed to the floor and I was almost knocked from my chair.

"The shields are holding," Dax said, confirming what I already knew. She sounded surprised.

"They are holding on all of our ships," Worf added. He was clutching his console as the *Defiant* continued to rock.

"Return fire, Mr. Worf," I said.

Instantly I could feel the surge of the laser fire. The

phaser cut a path ahead, catching a sweeping Mist ship like a bird in flight.

It exploded.

The Mist ship simply burst directly in front of us like a balloon stuck with a pin.

Our phaser had cut through it without any interference.

"What?" Prrghh said. "You've got to be kidding. Didn't they have a defense against your weapons?"

"They thought they did," Sisko said. "But they hadn't thought the situation through like we had."

"They hadn't modified their shields," the Caxtonian said.

"Exactly," Sisko said. "I'm not even sure they knew they had to."

"Okay," Prrghh said. "Explain this one."

"Sisko already has," Sotugh said.

"Explain it again," Prrghh said.

"I never realized that you were so slow," Sotugh said.

"And I never realized that you could be this rude," Prrghh said, sneering at the Klingon captain.

To forestall more fighting, Sisko said, "The difference between normal space and Mist space causes the shields to be slightly out of phase with the weapons. So they could have gone through our shields if we hadn't made the modification, and since they didn't modify their shields, our weapons went through theirs."

"And you wouldn't have known that if Captain Victor hadn't beamed through your screens when you first met," the Quilli said, obviously delighted at this turn of events.

"Exactly," Sisko said.

"So, I assume, you let Sotugh kill Captain Victor?" Prrghh asked.

"Sisko wouldn't do that," the wraith said. "Remember the argument about honor?"

"What did you do about Victor?" the middle-aged woman at the bar asked.

"And your ship?"

"And the Cardassians?"

"Well," Sisko said, feeling slightly overwhelmed by the questions, "you forget. The battle wasn't over yet."

A dozen other Mist ships exploded almost simultaneously, as the Klingon and Federation vessels returned fire. Debris flew everywhere. The scene was as devastating as the destruction of Jackson's ships. Jackson, by the way, pulled himself to his feet and watched, saying nothing. To this day, I do not know what he thought of that destruction.

Even though we were outnumbered two to one, the battle wasn't really a battle. They had no chance at all. Our weapons simply cut them apart while their weapons were useless against our modified shields.

It was an eerie battle as well. Imagine the Mist ships exploding in space, phasers and bright blue beams cutting through the darkness of space, and all around the devastation, other ships, Cardassian ships, hovered, as if nothing else was going on.

"To them nothing was," Sotugh said. "They were concentrating on *Deep Space Nine*. They could not even see us like we could see them."

"Exactly," Sisko said. "But we needed to pay attention to the coming fight, and with the mercifully short battle, we got our chance."

The fighting was over in a matter of seconds. Jackson looked stunned. The famed Grey Squadron of the Mist had been reduced to rubble in the time it took him to get to his feet.

"Nog," I said. "Open a channel to the starships and the Klingons."

"Aye, sir," he said. "Go ahead."

I stood. "Don't destroy Captain Victor's ship. Surround and hold it."

"I still think you should have let me kill him," Sotugh said.

"It would have made things easier," Sisko said. "But I didn't know that at the time."

"Even if you had known that," Sotugh said, "you would not have killed him."

"You're right," Sisko said. "That's not how Starfleet fights its battles."

* * *

And we fought this one by the book. The *Madison* and three Klingon ships, including the *Daqchov*, moved toward Victor's ship while the remaining Klingon ships chased the fleeing Mist ships, cutting them apart with ease.

All Captain Victor had to do was surrender. The battle was over. He had lost. It was clear to everyone, even Victor himself, I'm sure.

But the clarity made no difference. Captain Victor was not going to surrender. And even though it seemed at that moment that we could take him easily, Captain Victor had other plans.

He put them into effect immediately.

CHAPTER
18

"WHAT OTHER PLANS could he have had?" Prrghh asked. "He clearly had no options. He had no defense against your weapons; his fleet was being destroyed; Jackson had the sympathy of the Mist worlds—didn't he?"

Sisko smiled. "He did," Sisko said.

"Victor's plan was the plan of a fool," Sotugh said.

"A desperate fool," Sisko said.

"But sometimes," the Quilli said, climbing on the back of its chair, "desperate fools make dangerous enemies."

"True," the Trill said, placing one booted foot on the seat of the Quilli's chair. Sisko wondered if the Quilli even knew that the Trill kept saving it from falling over.

"Quite true," Sisko said, "and we were thinking like Captain Prrghh. Any rational man would know he had lost. Unfortunately, Victor was not rational."

* * *

He kept firing at us. The shots rocked the ship, but did no damage.

"What's he doing?" Jackson asked, as he held on to one of the consoles.

"I hoped you could tell me," I said. Victor's ship cut past the *Defiant,* shooting as it went. We rocked again.

"He's heading toward the station," Dax said.

"Screens holding at ninety percent," Worf said.

I stood. Perhaps Captain Victor had not understood what I had been saying to him. "Hail Captain Victor."

"I am hailing," Nog said, "but he's not responding."

"Open a channel anyway, Cadet, and broadcast this message to Victor on all frequencies. Ready?"

"Aye, sir," Nog said.

I nodded. "Captain Victor, cease fire or be destroyed with the rest of your ships."

In response, Victor shot at the *Defiant.* The bright blue beam hit our shields directly, and bounced harmlessly off them.

"I don't think he's going to surrender," Dax said.

"He's a fool," I said.

"You said you were going to destroy him," Jackson said, "but there are some good people on those ships who are simply doing their jobs. They don't know what's going on."

I knew that. It was that way in any war. That's why wars were so devastating. I did not answer Jackson, not then.

"The captain does not believe in unnecessary bloodshed," Worf said.

"I think taking out Victor would have been necessary bloodshed," Sotugh said.

"You could have done so," Sisko said.

Sotugh shrugged. "I figured it was your fight, Sisko."

Sisko looked at him, not entirely believing that. "The *Daqchov* flanked Victor's ship on the right, and the *Madison* flanked him on the left. . . ."

They flew in and around the Cardassian ships as if they were flying around posts.

Victor's ship headed directly for the station. For a moment I thought Victor was attempting to use the station as some sort of shield, even though it was in normal space and he was in Mist space.

Then a white line of mistlike clouds appeared near the station and expanded, flowing over the station like a bad storm over the top of a mountain.

"He's bringing the station back over," Dax said.

"You're kidding," the Trill said. "What about the Cardassians?"

"To them," Sisko said, "the station had yet again disappeared."

"I wish I could have seen the expression on their faces," Sotugh said.

Sisko grinned. He hadn't thought of that before. "So do I," he said.

"Imagine planning an attack on an outpost that winked in and out like a strobe light," the wraith said, laughing.

"There have been stranger things in this world," Arthur said cryptically.

"Did he think he could take over the station?" the Quilli asked. "Jackson had failed. What was his plan?"

"The plan of a desperate man," Sotugh said. "He seemed to be inventing it as he went along."

"And our team was matching him move for move," Sisko said, "invention for invention."

As the white mist cleared, and Victor's ship moved under one of the docking pylons, I told the cadet to hail Major Kira.

A moment later Kira's dirt-smudged face appeared on the screen. "Since there is now a Mist vessel on my screen, I assume we've been pulled back into their space."

She did not sound happy.

"That's Captain Victor's ship," I said. "We're trying to catch him alive."

"Someday you will explain this obsession with letting your enemies live," Sotugh said.

"And someday you can explain to me why you think death is preferable to a long life spent contemplating crimes," Sisko said.

Go on! several patrons yelled.

Sisko smiled. "I said to Major Kira . . ."

* * *

"Have you engaged the modification in your shields?"

She glanced down at her panel. "It'll be engaged in fifteen seconds," she said. Then she sighed. "You know, I wondered why you insisted we get those specs. Did you know he'd do that?"

"You once said, Major, that the best commander is the prepared commander."

She grinned. "So I did."

"Stand by," I said. "We'll return you to normal space as quickly as possible."

Her image disappeared from the screen. In front of me now, I could see the station, surrounded by the Cardassians, with Victor's ship near the docking pylons, the Klingons and the *Madison* also nearby, and all the debris from the destroyed Mist ships.

"The Cardassians are moving again," Cadet Nog said.

He was right. On the screen it seemed as if every Cardassian ship in the fleet had suddenly started to move at once, in all directions. The effect of the station disappearing from the midst of their ships had been like kicking an ant pile. The ants were scattering.

"I don't think Dukat would like to hear you compare him to an ant," Cap said with a grin.

"Fortunately he's not here," Sisko said with an answering grin.

* * *

Dax noticed the problem first. "The *Daqchov!*" she said.

I could see exactly what she was talking about. As the *Daqchov* had come around to flank Victor's ship, a Cardassian battle cruiser had suddenly, and without warning, turned and accelerated. The *Daqchov* didn't stand a chance.

Sisko waited for Sotugh to add something. It was, Sisko knew, a slightly dirty trick. This was probably the part that Sotugh did not want to discuss.

Sotugh took a long drink from his blood wine. Then he wiped his mouth with the back of his hand. When he looked up, everyone in the bar was watching him.

He scowled at Sisko, then said, "Those filthy Cardassian dogs went right through us. I could see their bridge. Almost smell their stench."

Everyone waited.

Sotugh said nothing else.

"That's not all that happened," Sisko prompted, knowing that the Klingons had felt the extreme dizziness and nausea just as his crew had when the Klingon ship had gone through them earlier.

Sotugh's gaze met Sisko's. In Sotugh's eyes, Sisko could see the memory of that horrible experience, but Sotugh shrugged.

"We felt a little discomfort," Sotugh said. "It was nothing to a Klingon warrior."

"It was enough to remember," Sisko said, grinning.

"The entire battle was strange enough to remember," Sotugh said. "That does not make it important."

"It would have been important if we had lost," Sisko said.

"But we didn't," Sotugh said.

"No," Sisko said, "we didn't."

"I would imagine," Dax said, "that the *Daqchov* is out of commission for a few minutes."

"I think you're right, old man," I said. "Is there any movement from Captain Victor's ship?"

"No, sir," Worf said.

"Let's try this again, Cadet. Hail Victor's ship."

"I'm hailing them, sir," Nog said, "but they are still not responding."

"He won't respond," Jackson said. "Not now."

"What makes you say that, Jackson?" I asked.

"I know Victor. He can be incredibly stubborn."

"Obviously," Dax muttered.

I shook my head. I had no respect for leaders who jeopardized their people in pursuit of a cause already lost. "Cadet, broadcast this on all frequencies. Ready?"

"Aye, sir."

"Captain Victor," I said. "There is nowhere for you to run. Surrender your ship now."

"Sir," Nog said, swiveling his chair. He looked surprised. "We have a response now."

"Uh-oh," Jackson said softly.

I ignored him as Captain Victor appeared on screen. His yachting cap was long gone, his hair stood up in tufts, and his uniform, which had been crisp before, appeared rumpled. He had a wild look in his eyes and beads of sweat dripped from his forehead. Councillor Näna was still beside him, but was no longer facing the screen. All I could see was his left eye rolling slowly in its socket.

"Sisko," Victor said, "I will blow up this ship and take your station with it."

"Oh," Prrghh said. "I hadn't thought of that one."

"It would have been a good option if his weapons worked against Federation defenses," the wraith said.

"Did he modify his equipment?" the Quilli asked, breathlessly.

"He didn't have time," Sisko said.

"So what did you do?" the middle-aged man at the bar asked.

I laughed.

Then I said, "The station's screens are adjusted for your space and are much stronger than any ship's. All you'll manage to do, Victor, is kill yourself and murder your crew. You don't want to do that."

Now the wild look in his eyes became even more intense and he cut off communications without another word.

* * *

Prrghh shook her head. "You laughed at an insane man?"

Sisko smiled. "I did," he said.

"Which only drove him crazier, I'll bet," the Trill said.

"The plan to take over an essentially peaceful people was insane from the start," Sisko said. "Being laughed at was the last thing he wanted."

"Sisko," Sotugh said. "You surprise me."

"I know," Sisko said. "I surprised Victor too."

Less than ten seconds after I had laughed at Captain Victor, his ship turned and cut away, firing randomly at the ships blocking him. None of them fired back, but they kept on his tail, flanking him.

"Dax, shift the station back to normal space," I said as Victor cleared the area. "Then follow him close."

"Transferring," she said.

The white line formed in space near the station, then expanded to a cloud that passed over the station.

"Transfer complete," Dax said. "The station has returned to normal space."

"Let's hope it stays there," I said as the *Defiant* turned. We headed after Victor's ship and caught up to it moments later.

He shot at us again, rocking us slightly as the bright blue beam bounced off our shields. Dax positioned the *Defiant* directly behind the Mist ship.

"Shields holding," Worf said.

"Madison and *Daqchov* are pacing Victor's ship on either side," Dax said.

"Where does he think he's going?" Jackson asked. "He has no way of escaping."

"He is insane," Worf said as if he were explaining to a child that space is a vacuum. "Do not ask for logic."

"Cardassians are again taking up attack positions near the station," Dax said.

"Major Kira is again warning them off," Nog reported.

I had had enough of Captain Victor. "Let's end this," I said. "Cadet, open a channel to Captain Victor's ship."

"Open, sir," Nog said.

"Captain, cease fire and come to a complete stop or be destroyed. This is not a bluff."

I motioned for Nog to cut the communications.

"So all this noble talk of allowing your enemy to live is just a lie," Sotugh said. "You simply wait until you tire of his antics and then you kill him."

"No," Sisko said. "I decided that Victor was a loose cannon. If we couldn't stop him, and quickly, he would cost other lives, especially with what was developing in normal space."

"That's certainly a reason to take someone out," the middle-aged woman at the bar said.

"It's called giving someone enough rope to hang

himself," the middle-aged man added. "We humans do that a lot."

"It is more efficient to kill the offender early so that time is not wasted in senseless pursuit," Sotugh said.

Sisko grinned at him. "Or so that the pursuers don't have a Cardassian ship sharing their position in out-of-phase space."

"I did not say that," Sotugh said.

"But if Sisko had taken out Captain Victor earlier, you would have missed that wonderful experience," Prrghh said.

"Believe me," Sotugh said. "It was worth missing."

"So did you catch him?" the Quilli asked, climbing even higher on his chair. The Trill had to put his other foot on the seat to keep the chair from tipping over. "Or did you kill him?"

"Captain Victor?" Sisko said. "I had Worf target his ship."

"Fire on my mark," I said.

"Ready, sir," Worf said.

With one final shot at the *Madison* that bounced harmlessly off its shields, the Mist ship suddenly stopped firing, slowed, and stopped.

"Well, that's a surprise," Dax said.

"A trick, sir," Worf said.

"Hold position and we shall see," I said.

"They are hailing us, sir," Nog said.

"On screen."

Councillor Näna appeared, his gray features dominating the screen. His mouth was opening and closing as it did before. Behind him, two humans were holding a struggling Captain Victor on the ground near an instrument panel.

Councillor Näna's mouth opened. "We," it said. Then the mouth closed. A second later, it opened again. "Surrender." Its eyes rolled forward toward me, and I realized just how hard it was for the councillor to speak aloud.

"Excellent," I said.

I turned to Jackson. He was watching Näna with his mouth open. When he saw me look at him, Jackson's mouth closed. Apparently he had never heard Näna talk before either.

I grinned at Jackson. "Do you have enough healthy personnel to take over and control that ship?"

"I do," Jackson said.

"Then it's all yours," I said.

"Thank you, Captain," Jackson said. For a moment, his gaze met mine. The respect, it seemed, was finally mutual. Then he quickly spun and headed for the door.

I turned back to Councillor Näna. "Jackson and some of the others will be taking control of your ship. Do not fight him."

Councillor Näna nodded slowly. Before the screen cut off, one of the men sitting on Captain Victor slugged him, knocking him out. Clearly Captain Victor's days of leadership were over.

* * *

"I had hoped for a glorious battle," Sotugh said. "Instead, I chased a few weak ships, shot our weapons a few times, and did nothing. The battle was without honor. We fought an enemy that looked powerful, but in truth, had nothing but weakness at its core."

"That's some story, Sisko," the wraith said, pulling its entire left hand. The Trill yelled a caution from the other side of the room. The wraith immediately flattened its hand against its chest.

"Yes, it is quite a story, despite Sotugh's disappointment," Prrghh said. "It reminds me of the time—"

"The story is not over yet," the Quilli said, waving its tiny paws. "How did the *Defiant* get back to normal space? Did you meet your time limit?"

Sisko smiled. "I am amazed at all of you. You have forgotten an important detail."

"And that is?" the Trill asked.

"The Cardassians," he said, "are still about to attack the station."

Sotugh slammed down his empty mug of blood wine. "That's right!" he said. "We still had to deal with those filthy Cardassian dogs!"

CHAPTER
19

"YOU DON'T SEEM to like the Cardassians much," the Trill said, with a slight smile playing on his face.

"They are a lying, duplicitous race, worthless in the extreme," Sotugh said. "They exist only to create trouble, and to spread their vileness throughout the quadrant."

"Sounds like Klingons to me," Prrghh said, moving just far away enough that Sotugh couldn't reach her.

"Actually," Arthur said, "Klingons have honor. They don't try to spread their vileness throughout the quadrant."

Sotugh nodded at him, in grateful acknowledgment.

"Could've fooled me," Prrghh said.

The Quilli was frowning again. "I thought you said that the Cardassians ran like—ents?—whatever those are. I thought you said they were gone."

"Ants," the Trill said, "an Earth insect, usually

about the size of your nose bristles. They live in colonies—the ants, not your nose bristles—often called anthills. When one is kicked, the ants scatter."

"How come you seem to know all this stuff?" the Quilli said to him.

"Because I *understand* stories," the Trill said, "instead of collecting them."

"Is he right?" the Quilli said. "About the ants?"

"Yes," Sisko said.

"Then they scattered. Or you used the wrong metaphor."

Sisko smiled at the small, fierce creature. "No, I didn't. Ants scatter, but sometimes they return to the nest, especially if their queen is inside. Sometimes they even rebuild that nest—"

"Which is a perfect analogy for Terok Nor," Sotugh said, "which is the Cardassian name for the Cardassian-built station *Deep Space Nine.*"

"It was theirs?" the Quilli said.

"Initially," Sisko said. "How we came to be in possession of it is yet another story."

"You won it in a war?"

"Not exactly," Sisko said.

"Wow," the Quilli said. "Another story. If this one ends like I think it will, I'll want to hear the others."

"Another time," Sisko said. "I am not done with this one yet."

"So," the wraith asked, "what happened when the station shifted back to normal space? What did the Cardassians do?"

212

"They saw the station's double disappearance and return as an opportunity," Sisko said. "And a weakness, especially with all the Klingon and Starfleet ships gone."

"Like dogs on a dying animal," Sotugh said. "Cardassians are nothing better than scavengers. We should have wiped them out when we had the chance."

"You want to wipe everyone out," Prrghh said.

"Some more than others," Sotugh said, glaring at her.

"When the station reappeared for the second time," Sisko said, "Gul Dukat must have been going slightly crazy himself, attempting to discover what was happening."

"Yes," Sotugh said. "Another hint as to his future."

"So," Sisko said, "he decided to take over the station and ask questions later."

"Typical Cardassian stupidity," Sotugh said.

"Captain," Worf said. "The Cardassians are in attack positions around the station."

This was the last thing I needed. I was tired of Dukat trying to take advantage of every situation that came his way. The man had lost *Deep Space Nine* years ago, but he had never gotten over it. I wished he would stop trying to take it back.

"Is the station able to defend itself?" I asked.

"According to my readings, it is," Dax said. "They have recalibrated the shields for normal space."

"But they will not last long with a full-out attack," Worf said. "There are too many Cardassian warships."

"Major Kira is warning them to stand down again," Nog said. "She is being very clear about it."

Kira was yet again going head to head with Gul Dukat. I think, in some ways, he was her greatest nemesis, the one person she could not seem to get out of her life, no matter how hard she tried.

"The Cardassians are not responding."

How unlike Dukat. He usually crowed over his battle plans. He was probably uncertain as to what sort of trick the Federation was playing on him now. I wished he would respond as he normally did. Then I would have known what sort of battle loomed before my crew.

I studied the mess I saw on the screen in front of me. An entire fleet of Cardassian Galor-class warships surrounded *Deep Space Nine*. In Mist space, invisible to the Cardassians, were three Starfleet starships and nine Klingon battle cruisers. If the starships and Klingon fleet got back to normal space before the Cardassians attacked, the odds would be in our favor. Dukat would not fight such a force. We would win without firing a single shot.

"Cadet," I said, "open a channel to the *Madison,* and *Daqchov* and connect in the rest of the Klingon and Starfleet ships."

"Open, sir," Nog said as the image on the screen changed.

Captain Higginbotham was in his command chair, the grease wiped from his skin. His eyes were bright, and he appeared to be exhilarated from the earlier battle.

Captain Sotugh was on the other side of the screen. He was looking a bit queasy—

"Klingons do not get 'queasy,'" Sotugh said.

"Dizzy, then," Sisko said.

"Klingons do not get—"

"Come on, Sotugh," Sisko said. "I know you felt the effects of that ship going through yours. Do you want to describe it?"

"I was looking a bit—off-balance," Sotugh said.

"I don't think that's better," the Trill said, with a laugh.

"It doesn't matter how he looked," the Quilli said. "What did he do?"

"Actually, it's what I did," Sisko said. "I told them . . ."

"The Cardassians are about to attack the station," I said.

"I already noted that, Ben," Higginbotham said. "Shift us back over. They'll think twice about it then."

"I hope so," I said. "Make the necessary adjustments to your shields and gather in this area."

Sotugh looked disgusted. "Someday we will take care of Cardassia, once and for all."

* * *

215

"But you haven't yet, have you?" Prrghh said.

"Bah," Sotugh said, moving his hand in dismissal. "They will run from us, tails between their sorry little legs."

"One story at a time, please," the Quilli said, and leaned even harder on its chair back. The Trill had to bend his knees to accommodate the shift in weight.

"At that moment," Sisko said to the Quilli, "I didn't care about the future either."

"Today," I said, "let's just concentrate on *Deep Space Nine.*"

"My ship will remain here to help you," Sotugh said. "Send the other Klingon cruisers back."

I hesitated for a moment, then said to Sotugh, "Adjust your shields anyway. In case we both have to cross back over quickly. Sisko out."

"You had no intention of letting me stay, did you?" Sotugh asked, his mood shifting suddenly. "You lied to me. Are you without honor, Sisko?"

"Honor, shmonor," Prrghh said. "I think we all know that Sisko has honor. Come up with a new accusation, Sotugh."

"Of course I wasn't going to let you stay," Sisko said. "The destruction of the Mist Grey Squadron was over and I couldn't deprive you of a good fight with the Cardassians."

"That is not why you sent me back," Sotugh said.

"Helping me with the Mist was not why you intended to stay," Sisko said. "You wanted the Mist's device."

"Of course," Sotugh said. "They had already crossed into our space once. Who is to say they would not do so again?"

"No one," Sisko said. "But we didn't need that device."

"You are not one to make decisions for the Klingon Empire!"

Sisko smiled. "At that moment, I was. I was the only one who controlled whether or not you remained in Mist space."

"And you sent me back."

"I sent you back," Sisko said.

"The Cardassians are powering their weapons," Worf said.

"Dax," I said. "Are the three starships in position, close enough to shift?"

"Yes," Dax said.

"Cadet," I said. "Warn them they have thirty seconds until we shift them."

"Aye, sir," Nog said.

"How about the Klingons?"

"Taking formation now," Dax said.

"I was a fool to listen to you," Sotugh said. "If I had not taken that position—"

* * *

"Good," I said to Dax. "Shift the Klingons as close together as possible."

"All of them?" Dax asked, glancing back at me.

"All of them," I said.

"You had no right, Sisko!" Sotugh said.

"I had every right," Sisko said. "This was my fight, from the beginning."

"Sisko's right," the Trill said. "The Intergalactic Rules of War have been the same throughout all of my lifetimes."

"There were devices floating in that debris," the wraith said. "Sisko said as much. You had a chance. You blew it."

"We were searching for devices," Sotugh said. "We did not find any."

"The story! Please!" the Quilli said.

"You can't change the past," the Trill said. "You may as well accept it, Sotugh."

"I accept it," he said. "I simply do not like it."

"Well," the Quilli said, focusing its beady eyes on Sisko. "What next?"

"Before we could transfer the starships," he said, "the Cardassians attacked the station."

They engaged in a full frontal assault, concentrating on the station's weak areas. Dukat knew where those areas were. He had been the head of the station for years. He might have even known the station better than I did.

What he did not know was that Kira had already sabotaged many of those weak areas, when the Mist had attacked. I knew that. And I knew that, if we did not hurry, Dukat would take over the station in no time at all.

Laser fire lit up as it hit the station's shields. Just as I had expected, Dukat was targeting the weak points in the station's defense systems.

"The station's shields are holding," Worf said. "But I do not know for how long."

"Get them help," I said.

"I'm transferring the starships," Dax said.

On the screen the white line of mist formed, then expanded into a large cloud covering the three starships, blurring their outlines. Then, as quickly as it had formed, it was gone.

"Transfer complete," Dax said.

All three starships instantly went into motion, moving with phasers firing at the attacking Cardassian ships. Once again, I was glad that Higginbotham was on my side.

"Transferring the Klingon fleet," Dax said.

The white cloud expanded, covering every Klingon ship for a moment before vanishing.

"Transfer complete," Dax said.

Even though I knew that Sotugh was surprised to be transferred back to normal space, he was thoroughly professional. He sent his ships directly into the battle, each ship focusing on a different Cardassian vessel.

* * *

"You are being charitable, Sisko," Sotugh said.

"I'm telling it as I saw it, Sotugh," Sisko said.

It felt very strange to just sit and watch a battle rage around us. It also felt strange to see Klingon battle cruisers and Federation starships fight Cardassian battle cruisers. I did not know then that what I was seeing was merely a taste of the future, of the battles we would find ourselves in a few months hence.

When I think of the beginning of that war, though, I do not think of the Dominion attacks or the agreement it made with Cardassia. I think of this moment, of the fleets fighting, because in some ways, this was the beginning.

Two minutes after the Klingons arrived, the Cardassians were retreating. They did not have the strength to battle Starfleet and Klingons. Not then. But this battle helped the Cardassians with future battle plans. Of that, I am now certain.

A number of their ships were heavily damaged. Dukat's flagship was leading the retreat.

Sotugh kept his ships in hot pursuit all the way to the Cardassian border, where they broke off the fight.

"Nice of the Klingons to help out like that," Dax said, breaking the silence of the bridge.

"It certainly was," I said.

CHAPTER
20

"How NICE OF YOU to acknowledge that," Sotugh said, sarcasm so great that Sisko half expected him to bow. "Here, at least."

"We acknowledged it there," Sisko said. "I'm telling you exactly what Dax said."

"I knew Dax as Curzon," Sotugh said. "He was rarely polite."

"You could say the same about Jadzia Dax," Sisko said. "She speaks her mind."

Sotugh inclined his head in Sisko's direction. It was, they both knew, Sotugh's way of letting bygones be bygones.

"So the story's over then," the wraith said.

"Weren't you paying attention?" the Quilli said. "The *Defiant* is still stuck in Mist space, perhaps permanently."

"It can't be permanent, or Sisko wouldn't be here," the middle-aged man said.

"You don't know that," the middle-aged woman said, jabbing him in the ribs. "For all we know, Sisko got his crew back to regular space and had to leave the *Defiant* behind."

"No captain would do that," Prrghh said.

"This place is a bit unusual," the wraith said, nodding toward Cap. "Perhaps Sisko came in from Mist space."

"I thought I was on Bajor," Sisko said.

"Blows that theory," the wraith said, shrugging. "So, how did you get the *Defiant* out? You had the only device on your ship."

"Not only that," Sisko said, "but we were nearly out of time. Even if we transferred the *Madison* back to Mist space, we would not have time to rig a device to her equipment."

The Klingons were after the Cardassians. There were other ships floating around *Deep Space Nine,* but none of them had the capabilities we needed. The debris from the destruction of Jackson's ships, and from the battle with the Grey Squadron, still drifted near us. The remaining Grey Squadron ships had not moved.

"Captain," Nog said. "Jackson is hailing us from Captain Victor's ship."

"Put him on screen," I said.

"Captain," Jackson said. "From the records on this ship, you were brought over to Mist space exactly one hour and fifty minutes ago."

"I know," I said. Getting us back to our own space

222

was the next thing I had to do. "We're running out of time."

"You may already be out of time," Jackson said. "Nothing has ever remained in Mist space this long and been able to cross back to normal space."

"My doctor says we have two hours and six minutes," I said.

"Well," Jackson said, "what your doctor, able as he may be, says, and what our experience tells us, are two different things. I'm not even sure you should try this."

"Would you?" I asked.

Jackson flashed me that charismatic grin. "I tried to get out of here for two full months after I arrived."

"Well, then," I said, "we'll start beaming over the last of your people in anticipation of our departure. Are you ready to accept them?"

"We are," Jackson said. "And don't forget to remove the shift device and any other material that belongs in Mist space."

"He did not want you to have the technology," Sotugh said.

"It was a precaution," Sisko said, "and more than likely it allowed us to shift. Dr. Bashir told me later that if any Mist item or person had been left on board the *Defiant*, we would not have shifted."

"Fine," Sotugh said. "Believe what you want, but I do not."

Sisko only shrugged and went on.

* * *

"I'll remember," I said to Jackson, and had Nog cut the connection.

I stood and looked at the screen for a brief moment. Despite the debris, and the few Mist ships still floating around the station, it looked normal. The Cardassian fleet was out of visual range, and so were the Klingons.

Deep Space Nine, at least, had gone back to normal. I hoped we could too.

I hit my comm badge, contacting the entire ship. "In exactly three minutes, Captain Jackson will shift us back to normal space. Every Mist resident and piece of equipment must be off this ship. This is priority one. Get to it, people."

"What exactly would happen if one of the Mist items remained?" the wraith asked.

"We weren't sure," Sisko said. "Beyond not being able to transfer. And just that was enough to worry me more than anything else."

"That must have been a scramble," Prrghh said. "Removing all that equipment and people."

Sisko smiled. "My crew is quite efficient," he said.

Dr. Bashir responded immediately. "Captain," he said. "You're going to have to beam most of these wounded directly out of sickbay. They're not yet able to go on their own."

"We'll beam them all," I said. "Make sure their clothes and every ounce of blood are either with them or in space away from the ship."

"Will do," Bashir said.

"Start getting Jackson's people out of here, old man," I said to Dax. "Put them on Jackson's bridge if you have to."

"Yes, sir," Dax said. "I have targeted their sickbay so that I'll be able to transfer the wounded directly."

"Do that first," I said. "I doubt you'll have time for any other precision maneuvers."

"You're probably right," she said, her fingers working her console as she spoke. Behind me, I could also hear Worf working. I knew that the other members of my crew were doing the same thing on different decks.

I hit my comm badge. "Chief, have you disconnected that shift device?"

"It'll take me at least ten minutes," he said. "If you want this ship working when it arrives home."

"I don't care if we're floating dead in space," I said. "You have two minutes. Do what you have to do."

"Yes, sir," O'Brien said.

I went to one of the consoles, and began beam-out work myself. I scanned the ship for foreign objects, using a parameter program that Dax had designed when she was looking for the shifting device in the debris. I found items scattered all over the *Defiant,* and I knew that other members of my crew were doing so as well.

I worked quickly—we all did—and because I was working quickly, I didn't have time to reflect. That was a good thing; I would have been worrying whether Dr. Bashir was right or whether John David Phelps

Jackson was right. I was hoping that Bashir was right, that we had the full two hours, but common sense told me that Jackson had the edge.

It concerned me that no one had left Mist space after spending this much time in it. It would be hard to see our world and not be able to interact in it. In fact, I have always believed that would have been the hardest part of all.

Watching, but never being able to even say hello.

"Benjamin," Dax said, "we have less than a minute."

I left my console and went back to my command chair, hitting my comm badge on the way. "This is the last warning, people."

"Ready, sir," Bashir's voice said through the comm line.

"Chief?"

"Twenty more seconds," O'Brien said. He sounded frantic.

"Cadet," I said, "connect me to Jackson."

"Aye, sir," Nog said.

According to Dr. Bashir's original calculations, we had two minutes left.

Within seconds, Jackson's frowning face appeared on screen. Behind him, I could see members of his crew crowding the bridge. "I think it has been too long, Captain," he said.

"My people assure me we have two minutes to spare," I said. "Are you ready to send us home?"

"Ready when you are," Jackson said.

"Do it quickly," I said.

"Captain," he said, bowing his head slightly, "thank you."

"You're welcome," I said, not at all graciously. We could forgo the niceties as long as the *Defiant* went back to her own space. "Now get us back where we belong and we'll call it even."

He nodded and the screen went back to showing *Deep Space Nine.* The station looked so close, and yet so impossibly far away.

"Everything's off the ship, Captain," Dax said.

"Very good, old man," I said.

At that moment, a white line formed directly in front of the *Defiant,* then expanded and moved back over the ship, covering us. I felt a slight twisting of my stomach, and space itself seemed to shimmer. My hands looked indistinct, and the bridge seemed to fade slightly.

Or maybe I only imagined that change.

I never checked.

Jackson's ship was gone.

"Well?" I said, my mouth dry.

"We're in normal space," Dax said, turning and smiling.

"Excellent," Worf said.

"Yes," Cadet Nog said, holding up a fist. "For a moment, I thought I would never see my father again."

"Or my son," I said softly. I had managed to avoid that thought throughout this ordeal, but now that it was over, I felt incredible relief, and I knew that my greatest worry had been leaving Jake forever.

Then, at that moment, something happened that I never would have expected. A white line formed in front of us, expanding into a cloud and covering the *Defiant*.

Suddenly Jackson's ship was there. And no one needed to tell any of us that we were again in Mist space.

"What did he do?" the Quilli asked, shaking its tiny paws.

"Was he as tricky as Captain Victor?" the middle-aged man at the bar asked.

"They couldn't have developed another crisis that fast," the Trill said.

"I know," the wraith said. "You snapped back because you had been there too long."

"No," Prrghh said. "They had to have brought him back."

"But why?" Robinson asked.

Sisko smiled at their reactions. They were remarkably similar to the reactions on his bridge. Sisko held up his hand for silence. "I'll tell you," he said.

"I do not like this," Worf said.

"Captain," O'Brien's voice came over the comm. "Is everything all right?"

"I'll let you know, Chief," I said. I stood, arms crossed. I hadn't even had a chance to get used to being in my own space.

"Jackson is hailing us, sir," Cadet Nog said.

"Put him on screen," I said.

Later, Dax told me I did not speak the words. I just growled them.

The screen filled with Jackson, and his crowded bridge. He was grinning that infectious grin, and his dark eyes twinkled.

I did not know how to react to that. So I asked the question I had planned. "Did something go wrong?"

"You returned just fine to normal space," he said, his grin growing as he spoke. "Your bodies were reset by the process. You again have two hours in Mist space."

"Wonderful," Dax said softly.

"Then what do you need us for?" I asked. "Is there some unfinished business here?"

"Actually, Captain, there is," Jackson said. "Since you had to leave in such a hurry, there was a group that wanted to thank you. And the only way they could do that was for me to bring you back across one last time."

Even as annoyed as I was, I smiled at that.

"Please stand by," Jackson said.

A moment later the screen filled with the images of six robed figures. They were egg-shaped and their skin was a filmy white, as opaque as fog yet as see-through as mist burning off on a summer morning. They had standard features, but they were distorted, almost as if they couldn't hold their shape. These six figures obviously belonged to the original Mist race.

* * *

"I thought Näna was part of that race," Sotugh said.

"I did too until that moment," Sisko said. "He was a member of some other race that had transferred over, just like the humans and the strange-looking Klingons."

"You may allude to that all you want," Sotugh said, "but I will not tell you about those Klingons. It is not something we discuss with outsiders."

"Did they really want to say thank you?" the Quilli asked.

Sisko nodded.

The nearest figure floated toward the screen. That is the only way I can describe his movement. It was too smooth to be a walk.

"Captain Sisko," the figure said. It had an androgynous voice with a bit of a quaver, as if it were speaking through water. "I am Councillor Ell-Lee of the Mist High Council."

"Pleased" was all I could think to say.

"We asked Jackson," Councillor Ell-Lee said, "to bring you back to our space one last time for two reasons. First, we would like to thank you for stopping Captain Victor and Councillor Näna. In thousands of years of Mist history, this is the first time something like this has happened. We are profoundly embarrassed."

"No need to be," I said. "We are sorry that it happened too, but we are glad that everything could be resolved."

"Embarrassment is a good emotion," Ell-Lee said. "It tends to stop a repeat of the same action."

I laughed. "True enough."

Ell-Lee smiled. Or, at least I think it smiled.

"So, Captain, from all of the council and the hundreds of worlds of the Mist that we represent, we thank you."

"You are quite welcome," I said, bowing formally.

Dax looked at me, a slight smile on her face. Later, she would tease me for my formal reaction. But this did seem to be a formal occasion. It isn't often that we get thanked for doing our jobs.

Ell-Lee's smile faded. It raised its hands. "Our second reason is a simple one. We would like you to take a message to your government, and that of the Klingon High Council."

"Gladly," I said.

"Please convey to your governments that such actions that happened today will not take place again. We have no hostile intentions with the Federation or the Klingon Empire and simply wish to be left alone."

"I will gladly relay that message," I said.

Ell-Lee bowed its head slightly. "And now, I must be, in the eyes of your culture, rude. But we have discussed it and we see no choice."

I braced myself. This was the reason they had brought us back. Things never were as they seemed with the Mist.

"Please tell your governments," Ell-Lee said, "that any attempt to contact us, or transfer into Mist space,

231

will be stopped at once. We have chosen isolation, and we prefer it. We will not be disturbed."

It was a clear warning. It was probably directed at me, and at my people, since we had gotten a hold of Mist technology and had a chance to study it before giving it back. The possibility existed that we could reproduce it.

"Do you think so?" Sotugh asked, suddenly interested.

Sisko did not answer him directly. But he looked at Sotugh as he said, "I told Ell-Lee that I would relay its warning. I did so at once to Gowron and now I have again."

Sotugh scowled and sat back.

"Good," Ell-Lee said, again smiling. "I am glad we are clear."

"Very clear," I said.

"Again, Captain," Ell-Lee said, "for all the Mist people, I apologize to you and your Federation. And to the Klingon Empire."

"We accept your apology," I said.

Ell-Lee lowered his hands and said, "Thank you."

And the screen returned to Jackson.

"I guess the council won't get caught like that again," he said with a sheepish grin.

"I hope not," I said, and then I smiled to take the sting out of my words. In truth, though, I did not want to come to Mist space again.

"Good luck, Captain," Jackson said. "And please accept a personal thank-you from me."

With that the screen cut back to showing the station.

A white line appeared in space and expanded, forming a cloud of mist that covered the *Defiant* for one last time.

A moment later we were again back in normal space.

CHAPTER
21

"EXCELLENT STORY," the Quilli said. It clapped its paws together. "My congratulations."

"Uh-oh, here it comes," the Trill said.

"What?" the middle-aged woman at the bar asked. "It *was* a good story."

Sisko smiled. "I really do not think I have time for another story—"

"We'll discuss that in a moment," the Quilli said. It jumped off its chair, landing on all four feet, its bristles sticking straight up. Then it gripped the leg of the chair, and pulled itself upright. It waddled toward Sisko

Sotugh stood. "Warthog, you and I have unfinished business."

The Quilli stopped waddling, and looked up at the Klingon. It had to look up so high that the weight of its head almost tipped it over backward.

"You and I have settled our business," the Quilli

234

said. "Your business is with that Trill. He lied to you. My bristles aren't poisonous."

"Is this true?" Sotugh bellowed.

Several patrons shrugged and looked away.

"Oh, dear," Prrghh said. "You've insulted the vaunted Klingon honor."

"Trill," Sotugh said. "You and I must settle this *now*."

The Trill stood. "I'd love to," he said. "But we can't fight in here, and I doubt we can fight out there. I suspect we entered in completely different places."

Sisko frowned at that, not completely understanding it.

"Another time, then," Sotugh said. He grabbed his mug of blood wine, finished it, wiped the back of his mouth with his hand, and then shook the wet hand at the Quilli.

Blood wine draped its bristles. It narrowed its eyes; several bristles extended and then receded. "I suppose you owed me that," it said.

"That's enough," Cap said.

Sotugh ignored him.

"Sisko," Sotugh said, turning to him. "You are a fine storyteller, but if you ever trick me in battle again, we shall settle the matter in a purely Klingon manner."

"It would be my pleasure," Sisko said. He picked up his Jibetian ale, and then paused. "Sotugh?"

"Yes?" Sotugh said.

"The same goes if you ever trick me. Do we have an understanding?"

"I think so," Sotugh said. "Until the next battle."

"Until then," Sisko said.

Sotugh nodded toward Cap and headed out the door. The gecko he had displaced climbed back onto the now-empty chair. The Quilli waited until he was gone before proceeding.

When it reached Sisko's feet, it stopped. "As I said," the Quilli said, "a fine story."

It extended a paw. After looking at it for a moment to see if it had any bristles (it didn't), Sisko took it. It was too tiny to shake, but that didn't matter. Apparently the Quilli wasn't going for a handshake. It wanted leverage.

It pulled Sisko's hand as it climbed up his leg, over his lap, and onto the tabletop.

"There," it said, its soft breath hitting his face. The creature smelled like cinnamon. "I have a business proposition for you."

"You've got to be kidding," the Trill said.

The Quilli straightened. "I don't steal my material."

"Then you're the first Quilli I've met who doesn't," the Trill said.

"Theft is not allowed in the Captain's Table," Cap said. "It's grounds for permanent expulsion. Captain Zzthwthwp knows that."

"Indeed I do, as do all Quilli captains," the Quilli said. "And so," it said, looking at Sisko, "because I am an honorable Quilli, and because that is such a fine story, and because I know it will have a great audience among my people, I am prepared to pay you twenty thousand zwltys for your tale."

The Trill stood. "Quilli make a minimum of ten thousand zwltys for every performance they give of a good story. I think you're underpaying the captain."

The Quilli smiled. "You didn't let me finish. Twenty thousand zwltys up front, against a ten-percent cut of the total sum of all the fees paid on the story's performance."

"Paid biannually," the Trill said. "And you could probably give him more than ten percent."

"There are costs involved," the Quilli said. "Rental of performance space, advertising—"

"Paid biannually at least," the Trill said.

"You didn't let me finish," the Quilli said. "Ten percent paid biannually, the first installment to come in the month of Shedding."

"What's that?" Sisko asked Cap, trying to hide his amusement.

"I believe, in Earth terms, it would be called October."

"Do we have a deal?" the Quilli asked.

This time, Sisko did let himself grin. Then he shook his head.

"He doesn't know how much a zwlty is," the wraith said. "Can you do the conversion for him, Cap?"

Sisko held up a hand to stop Cap's answer. "Unfortunately," Sisko said, "I cannot accept any monetary payment for my story. My people frown on that sort of thing."

"But I will retell this story!" the Quilli said. "It's

lodged in my brain!" It looked at Cap. "I thought I could pay for it."

"It looks like it would be theft," Cap said. "Guess you'll have to purge that one."

"It's too good to purge," the Quilli said.

"I do have a solution," Sisko said.

The Quilli frowned and sat down, rather like a spoiled child who wasn't getting its way.

"There is an orphanage on Bajor that I have sponsored. It is always in need of supplies and goods. If you would use my fee to provide for that—"

"I'm afraid that's not possible," the Trill said. "Captain Zzthwthwp has never been near Bajor, and probably will not be."

Sisko frowned. "But I—"

Cap held up his hand. "It's a long story, Captain. I will explain it to you later. But let's settle this first. If you and Zzthwthwp trust me, I will be the broker between you. I will make certain supplies and goods get to your orphanage in the correct time and place."

"That sounds fine to me," Sisko said.

"Me, too," the Quilli said. "So we have a deal?"

"How do you know he'll pay, though?" the wraith asked.

"That's where I come in," the Trill said. "Right, Zzthwthwp?"

The Quilli frowned. "You take all the fun out of everything."

"So you're a Quilli monitor?" the middle-aged man at the bar asked.

"Someone has to do it," the Trill said. "And I

happen to like good stories well told. I'll keep track of the performances and make sure that this little Quilli translates your ten percent into the proper number of supplies for your orphans."

"What's your cut?" the middle-aged man at the bar asked.

"I'll take one additional percent of the Quilli's profits."

"Hey!" the Quilli said.

The Trill crossed his arms. "It's either that or you don't get your story."

The Quilli rested its chin on its paws. "I hate it when you do that."

Sisko's grin widened. "It's a deal, then," he said. "You're welcome to the story, my friend."

The Quilli brightened. "I'll tell it exactly as you did," he said.

"Interruptions and all," the Trill mumbled.

Sisko took a final sip of his Jibetian ale. He was tired—a good tired—and he knew he'd better leave before the Quilli asked for another story.

"You're going?" Prrghh asked.

Sisko nodded. "I am on a short leave. I have to get back to *Deep Space Nine* soon, and I seem to have lost all track of time."

"Not surprising," Cap said, smiling. "You're welcome to come again, Benjamin Sisko."

"Oh, I will," Sisko said. "You make the best jambalaya I've had outside of New Orleans on Earth—aside from my own, that is." He extended a hand. Cap took it, and they shook.

"I will tend to your orphans," he said softly.

Sisko nodded. He believed Cap. He wasn't sure why, but he did. "I appreciate it," Sisko said.

As he wound his way around the chairs, other patrons clapped his hand, or smiled at him. As he passed the lizardlike humanoid near the piano, the creature raised its head and blinked ever so slowly at him.

Sisko felt a surge of appreciation. Or that's what it seemed like. That seemed to be the creature's way of telling him that he liked the story.

Sisko turned past the piano toward the tiny entrance. As he did, a woman entered. She looked harried, her short hair mussed. She was shorter than he was, but moved with an air of command. She looked familiar—very familiar.

Clearly her eyes hadn't adjusted and she walked past him toward the bar without noticing him.

He was already in the short hallway, with his hand on the door, before a thought registered.

As quickly as it did, he shook it away. It couldn't be. She had vanished years ago in the Badlands. No one had heard from her since.

If she were on Bajor, he would know it.

Besides, as long as he had known her, she had worn her hair long.

They said that everyone had a double somewhere in the universe. He must have just seen hers.

He shook his head, and pushed the door open, stepping into the heat of Bajoran twilight. How many

Jibetian ales had he had? He didn't know, and he really didn't care. For the first time in a long time, he had relaxed.

Bashir had been right. A few days of R&R were good. Now Sisko could return to his cabin and get a good night's sleep. He would tell Bashir when he returned—

Or maybe he wouldn't. No sense letting that doctor get too cocky. Bashir might try to pull something like this again sometime.

Sisko grinned and walked down the sidewalk, feeling better than he had in weeks.

Inside the Captain's Table, just moments after Sisko had walked toward the entrance, the Quilli jumped onto his chair. "You could have made him stay," the Quilli said to Cap. "I'll wager he had a dozen good stories in him."

"One was enough," Cap said. "In fact, you probably should refine it before you forget it. You have orphans to think of."

The Quilli frowned, jumped off the chair, and leaped onto the Klingon. The sound of their battle filled the bar, but most patrons simply ignored them, although some jumped in with glee.

A couple started down the stairs in the back. The woman was Klingon and the regulars recognized her as Hompaq. She had her arm entwined with that of a human male. He was shorter than she was, but seemed to measure up to her in presence. His dark brown eyes were made for laughter, and he had an infectious grin that made his charisma clear.

"You didn't tell me that story," she said as she led him down the stairs.

"There's not much to tell," he said.

"But to permanently capture Jem'Hadar," Hompaq said. "That's quite a risk."

"Not for us," the man said.

"I thought you weren't ever going to get involved over here in normal space again," she said.

His infectious grin widened. "We had a favor to repay," he said. "Besides, as we all know, sometimes wars are won in the details."

"And just how did you find your way to the Captain's Table?" a tall man asked her.

"I smelled fire. And trouble."

"Both bad things at sea. Please go on."

Captain Kathryn Janeway sipped at her coffee, then did as she had been asked.

Maybe it was just cabbage stew, she continued. Trouble and cooked cabbage smelled a lot alike.

Dark planets always made me uneasy. Humans had sixth, seventh senses. I'd learned to listen.

"This way," I said with an unnecessary beckon.

"Why that way?"

"I don't know."

The narrow street was wet with recent rain, and there was a sense of steam around us. Dim figures came and went from doorways, cloaked and unspeaking. My mind made something of it, but perhaps the downcast eyes and drawn hoods were only due to the night chill. I hoped so, but . . .

"Captain?"

Back to work.

I turned, and tripped on a faulty brick in the street—doors, windows, banners and signs spun, and so did I. All elbows, a knee—I tried to catch myself, failed, and Tom Paris caught me.

A clumsy captain. That's what every crewman wants to see—his elegant, sure-footed, universally competent captain taking a spill on a grimy street.

"Shall we dance, madam?" Paris's college-boy face beamed at me, backlit by a gauzy street lamp.

"Quit grinning, Lieutenant," I snapped. "Starship captains don't trip. And we *never* dance."

He smiled wider and arranged me on my feet, making me ponder courts-martial for a second or two. "I'm sorry, Captain, I just thought your injuries—"

"They're fine."

Another few steps padded away under our feet before I realized that my mood had completely changed. Caution had blended with intrigue. I could no more turn back than fly.

We were heading down an alley that made me think of old London's back ways, heading toward a corner and another street. I wanted to get there, but caution boiled up a certain restraint. A few seconds wouldn't matter.

A passerby now looked up and nodded greeting. So other moods had changed too?

"This place feels *really* familiar," I mentioned.

"I thought I was imagining it," Paris said. "No place in the Delta Quadrant can possibly look familiar to us, unless we double back on our course—"

"And we didn't do that," I abbreviated. "This place seems like an old movie to me . . . a Gothic mystery . . . one of those stories with the light in the castle tower and the woman in the diaphanous nightgown running across a moor, casting back a fearful glance . . ."

Paris bumped his head on a hanging sign. "Looks like a western to me."

Casting him a glare, I said, "Lieutenant, let's get around that corner."

"Aye aye, Captain."

An unexplained thrill ran down my arms as cobblestones kneaded our soles—Holmes, are you hiding there around the corner? Watson? Wet and foggy, yet cowled in city sounds and people's voices muffled behind shutters. There were no horses hooves or wagon wheels—this culture was beyond that—but I found myself listening for a clop and clatter. The smoke-yellow street lamps were electrical, but inadequate. I had a feeling not of neglect, but purpose. Just a feeling . . . nothing but a feeling . . .

Usually feelings didn't so completely guide me.

Usually I depended upon rationality, upon keeping feelings reined hard, for they were inaccurate and undependable. Not *how do I feel?* but *what do I think?*—that's what guided me, and so far it had kept us all alive. Feelings were too susceptible to fears, and fear was a daily diet on this unending mission. And feelings were too sudden.

Even good feelings had been reined in a long time ago. I enjoyed a few things, but always kept control and never let myself enjoy too much. I never went over the top and forgot where we were and why. This kind of restraint, for a human being—a human woman—was unfortunate and even unnatural, but serviceable for me. If I kept my feelings in their place, good and bad, then I could handle the truly awful.

Like these last few days. Truly . . .

Just as I cast off my thoughts as beginning to be a little too Vulcan, I realized the voices we were hearing had gotten notably louder now that Paris and I had rounded the corner. Nothing raucous—just easier to hear, even to delineate individuals. Somebody was having a pleasant time. Down the street, there was a rowdier place, somewhere.

There were several doorways, each with some kind of hawker's sign swaying gently over it. When had a breeze come up?

I came to the first door on the left, snuggled into a leathery wooden archway by a good meter, and the heavy aged-oak door was propped open by what looked like an iron bootscraper. There was music, and a heady scent of fire and food—my memories stirred and pushed me toward the door.

"Tavern of some kind." I looked up at the dreary wooden sign and the carved letters.

"The Captain's Table . . ."

"Sounds nice," Paris commented.

I peered briefly at the faded paint, the four stars in each corner of the sign. "Very nice, Tom. But why is it written in English?"

He eyed the sign again. "English . . ."

How easy it was to forget that we were light-millennia away from anything English. When he looked at me again, his eyes bothered me. He wanted answers.

"Let's go in," I suggested.

Shivering through the eerie moment, Paris stepped closer. "Right behind you. Unless you want me to scout the rest of the street—"

"I don't know yet," I said. Besides, he didn't really want to go.

The wooden door wouldn't open without my shoulder involved. The wood was warm from inside, but dank on its surface from the fingers of fog slipping under the archway. I walked down a short corridor, which guided me into a left turn, through a second archway with darkened timber and a whiff of sea rot. As I turned, the Captain's Table tavern opened before me.

A warm, smoky cloak wrapped my shoulders and took me by the waist like an old friend's arm at a fireside, coddling me into the clublike environment of a country pub. To my left, there was a piano, but no one was playing. Its rectangled rosewood top sprawled like a morning airfield, reflecting incarnated gaslight from sconces on the paisley-papered wall. Before me was a raft of round tables; at the tables were people. Beings. Mostly men, a few women—most looked human, but there were some aliens. They sat in wooden armchairs worn to a warm grouse-feather brown.

Over there, to the right along the wall was a glossy cherrywood bar with mole-skin stools. The age-darkened bar laughed with carved Canterbury Tales-type figures. Over a mirrored backsplash a shelf was crammed with whiskey jugs, ship's decanters, and every manner of bottle. Over the bar and bottles glowered a huge Canadian elk head with a full rack, which threw me for a moment because it was so undeniably of Earth. I looked down at my uniform, expecting to see an English shooting suit. If I looked out a window, would I see hedgerows and pheasants?

I might see England, except that the image would be rippled by the occupant of a majolica bowl on the piano . . . a lizard? At first I thought it was part of the design on the bowl, but no, it was a real live gecko, a mottled yellow-green chap with two-thirds of a tail, and he was enjoying feasting on the conch fritters in the bowl. I would've warned somebody that a creature had crawled in, except that several people from a table over there were watching the gecko and commenting on the length of its re-growing tail.

A British pub in the Delta Quadrant with conch fritters and a live-in lizard. Hmmm . . .

There weren't any windows. There was draped fabric, with what looked like a tartan print, pulled back by silver brooches with amber and purple stones, but no windows behind any of it.

Many of the people glanced up—some nodded, others raised their glasses to me, and still others glanced, then ignored me further. A young man in a cableknit Irish sweater, with longish ivory hair and a voice like a Druid ghost's, softly greeted: "Captain."

How did he know?

As I paused and returned his look, I noticed that there was glass crunching under my boot. As the company turned for their own look, a lull in the general movement of the place made me notice what they'd been doing—that several people were scooping up spilled food and righting toppled glasses and chairs. Here and there someone was nursing a bruised face or a bleeding lip. There'd been a fight.

Then a fellow wearing a maroon knit shirt with a sailing ship and scrolled lettering embroidered on the left chest, nodded and invited, "Welcome aboard, Captain. Relax. We'll have it all cleaned up in no time."

Beside him, a large creature, with a mirrored medallion on his chest and a set of antlers rivaling the elk's on his head, nodded elegantly as the lamplight played on the hollow bones of his face. He was demonic, yes, but still somehow welcoming. I didn't feel threatened at all. Even my instincts were voiceless.

The embroidery on the shirt didn't really surprise me—if a planet had water and wind, there were also some sort of sailing vessels. Common sense of function demanded certain designs, just as telling time and traffic control had a certain universal sense that could be counted upon just about everywhere. There were only so many ways to run an intersection.

But the two who had spoken were clearly human and shouldn't have been in the Delta Quadrant at all. My crew and myself were the only humans in the Delta Quadrant.

I rotated that a couple of times in my mind, until I finally didn't believe it at all. *Most* of these people looked very human indeed, though quite a range of types—not unusual, for a tavern in a spacelane, in a populated sector with civilized pockets.

"My crew was a mixture of types from all over," someone was saying—a young man's voice, but without the flippancy of youth. I looked at the nearest table, and saw several people listening intently to a small-boned young man in a blue jacket with red facing running down the chest. His white neckerchief was loosened, and though he seemed relaxed, he also seemed troubled by his own story.

"The ship wasn't even ours. It was a converted merchantman on loan to us. Many of her timbers had rot in them, and though we possessed forty guns, several of those were inoperative. It was in the afternoon that the enemy closed on us, and the breeze was fading. We would soon be outmatched *and* crippled. On our last move, the enemy's sprit caught our mizzen shrouds—"

"Oh, my," someone uttered, and half the company shuddered with empathy.

The young man nodded somewhat cheerily at this. "Yes, but I lashed it there. Why not? I thought my ship would sink otherwise, and I wanted to fight! So I lashed up to something that would keep me afloat. My enemy's ship."

The table's company laughed in awed appreciation. I nudged a little nearer to keep listening.

"And I got it, by God, I got it," he said, shaking his head in the reverie of a rugged moment. "Their shots passed straight through the timbers of our gun deck as if going through a straw mattress. They invited me to surrender before the action became a slaughter. They had this odd conception that we didn't have it in us to establish ourselves as a power with which to reckon. But I'd hardly begun. I turned and simply told them such. My crew was so enthused that my riflemen in the tops dispatched the enemy's helmsmen one by one, and then a brisk fellow of mine vaulted the yards and dropped a grenade into the enemy's magazine. Such a roar! Their sails were lit afire!"

"And you were still made off to them?" the fellow in the maroon shirt asked.

I stopped moving forward, because I was now listening to the dark-eyed young officer in the blue coat with red facings.

"Oh, yes," he answered. "If they sank, they would drag us down. I had only three guns left and kept shooting. But the other captain's ship was a goner and he soon struck. *Serapis*'s crewmen were well thankful to offboard their vessel, you might well understand. A sinking wreck is bad enough, but a sinking *and* burning wreck soon becomes legend. We unlashed, and off we limped. Our entire gun deck was gone."

An unfamiliar alien standing nearby asked, "So you won? Or you lost?"

The officer craned around for a glance at the questioner, saw that this creature might be someone who wouldn't or shouldn't already know the answer, and offered, "My opponent's ship was a brand-new warship. Mine was a half-rotted old merchant. My ship sank shortly thereafter his, but his was the costlier loss, and we denied the enemy domination of vital commerce and supply lanes."

The young captain took a sip from a horn-shaped mug that looked like pewter. He sank back a bit in his chair and stared at the tabletop, seeing something quite else. "I heard later that the other captain had been made a knight for that action. I told my men that if I ever met him again, by God, I'd make him a lord!"

Everyone laughed again—and so did I—and somebody, a woman, commented, "You're a brat, John."

The young man nodded. "Oh, thank you."

Someone else said, "That's a pretty fair story. Too short, though."

"It seemed rather lengthy at the time. I'll be longer winded from now on."

"Do that. Short stories are for musers, not doers."

For a moment the conversation died down and I heard other things. Faint music from somewhere, but not from the piano . . . dueling pistols on a wall plaque, castle torchères, coach lamps and railroad lanterns, a shelf with little unmatched stone gargoyles, a huge Black Forest cuckoo clock with a trumpeting elk carved on top of flared oak leaves and big pulls in the shapes of pine cones . . . devil-may-care patrons huddled around the tables like provocateurs in a novel, and a large silver samovar that needed polishing . . . this place boggled the mind with unexperienced memories. Was I hearing the groan of oak branches and waves against a sea wall? The mutter of robber barons plotting in a back room? It was all seductively Victorian, and I felt right at home.

In a fireplace real wood burned—and somehow from it came the earthy aroma of autumn leaves like my grandfather had heaped up and burned outside the big farmhouse every October. He hadn't been a farmer, but he had a good time pretending.

Keeping my voice down, I turned my face just enough to speak over my shoulder to Paris. "This place looks like the Orient Express stopped at a Scottish pub in the Adirondacks. This isn't *like* Earth, Tom . . . this *is* Earth." He didn't respond, so I added, "I wonder if there's a back door to home. Somebody here has been to the Alpha Quadrant. Maybe they can show us their shortcut. Give me your tricorder."

I put my hand out, still looking around the pub, but Paris didn't give me his tricorder. Irritated that he could be so stupefied, I swung around to snap him out of it and found that he wasn't behind me anymore.

"Paris?" I called back toward the hooded entrance, but he didn't come out. I went to the archway and looked down the musky corridor to the street door, but he wasn't there.

I turned back to the pub again and looked around, taking more care to check each person, each being. A pale-haired man, very thin and not tall, stood at the bar, dominating a group of others who were listening to him. His dark uniform coat, lathered with ribbons and medals, had a high collar and tails, and the right sleeve with its thick cuff was pinned up to the coat's chest—that arm was missing at the shoulder. He certainly wasn't Lieutenant Paris, and neither were any of those around him.

Down the bar a stool or two were some men in naval pilot coats and sea boots. I found myself surfing the walls for a portal back in time, and *way* off in space.

I looked up a set of worn wooden stairs with a spindled railing, but there was no sign of Paris.

Had he gone back to the street? Why would he?

I turned to go out, but someone caught my arm. I looked—a young man had me by the arm. Human. Five feet eleven, if I reckoned right . . . and if I was Kathryn Janeway, that was a United States Marine uniform. A captain. A flier. He smiled, and there was a very slight gap between his front teeth that gave a

253

homey appearance to his narrow face, with its green eyes slightly downturned at the outside corners.

"Have a seat with us, Captain?" The Marine turned, not letting go of my arm, to a group of people at one of the larger tables, and he gestured to the nearest man. "Josiah, make room for the lady."

"Actually, I've lost track of my crewmate—"

"That's how it works at the Captain's Table. Don't fret over it. He'll be fine."

Annoyed, I peered briefly at the person who'd spoken, pausing in the middle of a dozen thoughts and wondering if she was really a captain, as everyone here seemed to be. She wore a plain knit turtleneck sweater, olive green, with three little crew pins on the collar, too small to read from here. She was unremarkable-looking, average in most ways, yet self-satisfied, and had a bemused confidence behind her eyes that said she'd crewed a few voyages. Beside her was a pleasant-faced Vulcan—which pummeled the lingering theory that I was imagining the Alpha Quadrant elements. He had typically Vulcan dark hair, but swept to one side instead of straight across the forehead, and he wore a flare-shouldered velvet robe with a couple of rectangular brooches. Whether for rank or ceremony, I couldn't tell. He motioned for me to take the chair they'd cleared, and the woman in the olive sweater nudged a little birch canoe full of walnuts toward me, showing a flesh-colored fingerless glove on her right hand. Looked like an old injury, but it didn't seem to bother her.

The man called Josiah, older and more grizzled

than most others in the knot of patrons at this table, was standing and offering me his chair. "Right here, madam."

Smoldering aroma of burning leaves . . . the musky scent of old wood . . . the comforting nods and touches of the people around me, the music, the elk head, the paisley wallpaper . . . I felt so much at home that I lowered myself into the chair in spite of having a crewman now missing. I lowered myself cautiously, because I felt there was still the chance another part of me would go through the chair.

". . . and that, my friends, is how I come to be sitting here with you, sipping this excellent coffee."

Standing over her, the man called Josiah turned toward the bar and called, "Cap! Shake the reefs out, man! Let's have those mugs here while there's still a beard on the waves!"

Janeway had no idea what that meant, but she liked the sound of it. *Well, my hand didn't go through the table, at least.*

A tall man with white breeches and a double-breasted blue jacket left the clique around the one-armed man at the bar and approached our table. He had a deep voice, uncooperative dark hair, and he was irritatingly proper in his manner. "Captain, welcome to our little secret," he said. "Care for a game of whist?"

"Not right now . . . Captain," Janeway said, daring the obvious while she tried to place his jacket in time and came up with about 1830. Maybe earlier. Noncommittally she added, "Just getting the feel of the place."

"It takes a moment for the logical mind," this tall man said, and pulled a chair up to the table for himself, tapping a set of playing cards on the table, then leaving the stack alone. Nobody else seemed to want to play cards, and he didn't seem willing to push.

"There's a record of places like this," I mused. "The planet in the Omicron Delta region . . . people see what they feel like seeing. Relive fond memories, great victories—"

"Or make new ones," the Vulcan said. Now the cloud of dimness rose a little more before my eyes and I noticed that under the sleeveless velvet and satin panels of his ceremonial robe he was wearing a red pullover shirt with a black collar and gold slashes on the cuffs. It looked familiar . . .

In the flood of familiarity and comfort here, I dismissed the nagging hint.

The man who wanted to play cards sat rod-straight opposite me—how could he be sitting and still be standing?—and in the fingers of yellowish lamplight I could now see that his uniform was weathered, even frayed at the shoulders, and there was a little hole on one lapel. This didn't bother the others at the table or short him any of their respect as they turned to him while he spoke, and that told me something about him. So I listened too.

"This place has a mystical characteristic which newcomers find boggling," he said. "Certainly I did.

It took the better part of my next voyage to dismiss the Captain's Table to a bad bottle."

"Magic comes hard to the organized mind," the Vulcan said.

Janeway looked at him, a little amazed. Vulcans didn't buy into mysticism any more than she did. She saw in his expression that she was right—he was much more amused than serious. The woman in the olive sweater smiled and nudged the Vulcan as if he were being naughty. What an unlikely couple. They obviously knew each other very well, and she got the idea they always sat together.

"I don't believe in magic," she told them. "There's obviously some bizarre science at work here. I've seen—"

The dark-haired officer's thick brows came down. "You name this science, your ladyship!"

Janeway paused, waiting for a laugh at his calling me that, but no one laughed. Not even a chuckle. I sensed the lack of humor was something about him more than something about me.

"Once upon a time," she answered, "people thought fire was of the gods. We thought the stars were Heaven. Then we made fire for ourselves and went to the stars. We learned there's no true alchemy, no 'magic' that can't be mastered eventually, but just science we haven't figured out yet." She glanced around again and sighed. "It's funny . . . I don't really want to figure this out. It looks like Earth, but . . . it's an Earth I'd make up myself. And that can't be real."

"Real enough, Captain," another voice interrupted.

It was the elegant officer with the tailed coat and the medals and the missing arm. He now turned from the clique at the bar, most of whom followed him as he approached our table. "The competent commander takes events as they come and acts upon the dictates of duty."

"Duty often fails to proclaim its requisites before the crucial moment, your lordship," the Vulcan said.

The woman in the sweater grimaced and chided, "That's it—lip off to a historic luminary. Brilliant."

"It's 'an' historic," he dashed back fluidly. "Like 'an' horse."

"Or 'an horse's ass.'" The woman looked at her again. "Don't try to figure it out all at once. You'll just end up sitting in a corner making sock monkeys."

The Vulcan made one elegant nod. "I have seven myself."

Janeway squinted at him. Was this all a show by some benevolent traveling theater group?

"I think the captain should tell her first story right now," the woman went on, looking at me again. "No point wading through hot air we've already heard, right? Dive, dive, dive—"

"Perhaps," the Vulcan said to his cocky tablemate, *"you* would like to regale us with one of your tales of grand heroism. The time you sat on the barkentine's deck at dawn, cracking thirty dozen eggs for the crew's breakfast and feeding the drippings to the ship's cat. Or the time you fell off the trader's quarterdeck step while carrying a can of varnish—"

"They were defining moments," the woman nipped.

Janeway was about to politely decline the invitation to relive one of the many tense and disturbing incidents that had happened to her and her ship since the accident that dropped them all in the Delta Quadrant, when yet another blast of incongruity appeared at the entry arch.

Pushing to her feet, she hissed, "That's a Cardassian!"

My arms were clutched from both sides and I was pulled back into my chair.

"A Cardassian *captain*," the Vulcan said. "All captains are given entry here."

Trying to get the pulse of this place, she buried what she really wanted to say and instead pointed out, "That can be its own kind of problem. It's one thing to club with other captains. It's something else to ask captains to club with those who have attacked our people and killed our shipmates."

They all fell silent at my words. They eyed the Cardassian just as I did. Had each of them seen an enemy captain in this place? Had that been the cause of the bar fight they were now pushing out of the way?

The fact that they didn't argue with me was revealing. They were captains. Loyalties, emotions, and a sense of purpose tended to run deep among those who had held in their charge the lives of others, in such intimate conditions as a vessel. And more, many here must have defended innocents from various aggressors—Janeway saw that in their eyes and heard it in their silence. None of them wanted to tell her she was wrong.

Given entry, he had said. Not *were welcome.*

Suddenly I thought this place a lot more interesting.

"Did you get another command, Captain?" the Vulcan asked the man who had told the story.

"Yes," John said, and his gaze fell to his hands cupped around his mug. "Yes . . . but one is most definitely not the same as another."

"That's hard on the heart, I know, John," the woman said to the man who had told the tale. "To move on to another ship after the one you love is destroyed."

Janeway found herself moved to add, "Somehow we find it in ourselves to move on if we have to."

"Have you 'had to,' Captain?" the Vulcan asked, his hazel eyes gleaming almost mischievously.

Janeway nodded.

"Go ahead," John invited, pushing a frothing mug toward her as several were delivered to the table. "Tell your tale . . ."

**To be continued in
Star Trek: The Captain's Table
Book Four: *Fire Ship*
by Kathryn Janeway
as told to Diane Carey**

Captain Benjamin Sisko
By
Michael Jan Friedman

His Early Life and Career

Benjamin Sisko was a devoted family man who grew up in New Orleans on Earth. His father, Joseph Sisko, was a gourmet chef of Creole descent who ran a small bistro in New Orleans.

The elder Sisko insisted the family dine together, so that his "taste testers"—his wife and two children—could sample his new recipes. This love of cooking, particularly with regard to his native Creole dishes, manifested itself in young Ben as well, allowing him to become an accomplished chef in his own right later in life.

While Sisko's sister moved to Portland, Oregon, the future captain himself attended Starfleet Academy in San Francisco. He distinguished himself there as a promising command officer.

Sisko met Jennifer, his future wife, at Gilgo Beach on Earth in 2353, just after Sisko's graduation from the Academy. After a short courtship, during which

Jennifer expressed reservations about marrying a Starfleet cadet, she and Sisko married. The couple had a son, Jake, in 2355.

Early in his Starfleet career, Ensign Sisko was mentored by Curzon Dax, a Trill whom he met at Palios Station. The two later served on board the *U.S.S. Livingston* together and remained friends for nearly two decades. Curzon Dax was in the habit of assigning Sisko the duty of escorting VIP guests so the Trill wouldn't have to deal with them.

Sisko also was friends with Calvin Hudson, a fellow Starfleet officer with whom he had attended the Academy. Sisko was sorely disappointed when Hudson later turned out to be a member of the infamous Maquis rebellion.

One of Sisko's earliest Starfleet experiences was a stint in the war between the Federation and the Tzenkethi. He served aboard the *U.S.S. Saratoga* as executive officer with the rank of lieutenant commander until early 2367, when the ship was destroyed by the Borg in the battle of Wolf 359.

Though Commander Sisko and his son survived the destruction of the *Saratoga,* his wife, Jennifer, tragically did not. Sisko was devastated by the loss, which caused him to withdraw into himself for a time and shun the idea of serving again on a starship.

Out of respect for his personal tragedy, he was assigned to the Utopia Planitia Fleet Yards on Mars, where he spent three years overseeing starship construction. One of Sisko's projects at Utopia Planitia included design work on the experimental warship *Defiant,* which he would later command.

However, Starfleet had no intention of letting such a valuable officer languish for long at Utopia Planitia. Sisko was eventually promoted to full commander and assigned to station *Deep Space Nine*—a former Cardassian facility near the planet Bajor, which had been occupied and exploited by the Cardassians for several decades.

On Deep Space Nine

Commander Sisko was not at all pleased with his posting to *Deep Space Nine,* as it didn't seem like the ideal place to raise a young boy. In fact, he was seriously considering civilian life as an alternative.

He also was not pleased with the officer who turned over the "keys" to the place—Captain Jean-Luc Picard, of the *Enterprise.* After all, the last time Sisko had seen the man was at Wolf 359—where Picard, as the Borg named Locutus, coordinated the Borg attack that resulted in the death of Jennifer Sisko.

However, after the Bajoran wormhole was discovered, the commander came to understand the strategic importance of *Deep Space Nine* and the challenge of bringing Bajor into the Federation—and rose to the challenge. He even overcame his negative feelings toward Picard in order to continue his role as Starfleet's presence on the station.

Among Sisko's staff at *Deep Space Nine* was science officer Jadzia Dax, a Trill who carried the memories and experiences of Curzon Dax. Sisko initially found it difficult to relate to his old friend in the body of a beautiful young woman, but the two eventually came to renew their friendship.

Shortly after his posting to *Deep Space Nine,* Sisko made contact with the mysterious life-forms identified as Bajor's legendary Prophets. These beings existed in the Celestial Temple—also known as the Bajoran wormhole—which was located in the Denorios Belt. Their nonlinear perspective on existence helped Sisko come to grips with the loss of his wife.

As a result of his contact with the Prophets, Bajoran religious leader Kai Opaka indicated that Sisko was the Emissary described in ancient prophecies as the one who would save the Bajoran people. Sisko was uncomfortable with his role as Emissary for some time, but felt obligated to respect Bajoran religious beliefs.

From the time of his wife's death, Sisko was reluctant to form another romantic relationship. It wasn't until 2370 that he took an interest in a mysterious woman called Fenna, who bore a strange resemblance to the wife of a scientist visiting *Deep Space Nine.* Much to Sisko's dismay and disappointment, Fenna turned out to be a mere psychoprojection created by the scientist's wife under stressful circumstances.

Sisko's next relationship had its share of rough spots as well. In 2371, he began dating an attractive freighter captain named Kasidy Yates, who shared his love of baseball. Their relationship blossomed rapidly into a serious love affair.

Thus, Sisko felt betrayed when Yates was exposed

as a Maquis sympathizer, who was helping to smuggle supplies into the Badlands. He confronted Yates with his knowledge of her activities, after which she gave herself up and served time in a Federation penal colony. As he had promised, Sisko was there for Yates when her sentence was over.

It was also in 2371—specifically, stardate 48959.1—that Sisko was promoted to the rank of captain, in recognition of his accomplishments on *Deep Space Nine*. Though rank had never been particularly important to Sisko, his subordinates thought the promotion was long overdue.

Commanding *Deep Space Nine* brought Sisko his share of difficult decisions. In 2370, for instance, a proto-universe threatened the safety of his station, but he refused to arbitrarily destroy the proto-universe. He felt that to do so would have been to act with the same indifference to life that the Borg had shown to the Federation.

In 2371, Sisko was abducted by a man who appeared to be Miles O'Brien, *Deep Space Nine*'s chief of operations. This man turned out to be the Miles O'Brien of the mirror universe originally discovered by Captain Kirk. The mirror O'Brien wanted Sisko to help a Terran rebellion, to fight an interplanetary group of oppressors known as the Alliance.

Sisko was disconcerted to learn that the counterpart of his late wife, Jennifer, was still alive in the mirror universe. It was Sisko's difficult job to convince the mirror Jennifer to abandon her work for the Alliance, and to persuade her to instead join the

Terran rebellion. Fortunately for the rebellion, he succeeded.

The captain entered the mirror universe again a year later, following his son after Jake was lured there by the living counterpart of his late mother. By then, the Terran rebellion had built its own *Starship Defiant*, but was having trouble making the warship operational—and needed Sisko's help to fend off an oncoming Alliance fleet.

Helping to get the *Defiant* shipshape, Sisko subsequently volunteered to lead its rebel crew into battle. His leadership enabled the rebels to emerge victorious—but not before the mirror Jennifer was killed, leaving Sisko and his son to deal with Jennifer's loss a second time.

In 2371, an automated Cardassian self-destruct program was accidentally activated on *Deep Space Nine*. Sisko, trapped in an ore-processing bay with his son and Miles O'Brien, risked his life to reach a control junction and successfully redirect the destructive force into space.

The Dominion and Other Foes

Sisko's greatest challenge as commander of *Deep Space Nine* was the threat posed by the Dominion, a powerful and hostile alliance of planetary groups in the Gamma Quadrant. The Dominion had been established by the mysterious and reclusive Founders, who were almost never seen, though a species of brutal soldier called the Jem'Hadar savagely ensured compliance with the Founders' rule.

Sisko first encountered the Dominion during a father-son bonding trip to the Gamma Quadrant, during which he ran into a group of Jem'Hadar. Some time later, hoping to avert a Dominion invasion by demonstrating the Federation's peaceful intent, Sisko took the newly commissioned *Defiant* and his officers into the Gamma Quadrant to find the Founders.

It turned out the Founders were shapeshifters, like Sisko's *Deep Space Nine* security chief, Odo—and that they were unlikely to accept the idea of a peaceful coexistence with the Federation. Sisko and his people returned to the Alpha Quadrant, sobered by the knowledge that war with the Dominion might be inevitable.

A year later, evidence that the Founders were targeting Earth for invasion sent Sisko back to his home planet, where he and Odo had to prevent—or prepare for—war with the Dominion. However, the more immediate threat was a Starfleet plot to wrest control of the Federation to better defend it against the Dominion. Sisko exposed the conspiracy and restored order on Earth, refusing to let fear conquer his homeworld for the Dominion.

In 2373, Sisko, Odo, and O'Brien disguised them-selves as Klingons and joined Commander Worf, formerly of the *Enterprise*-D, on a suicide mission into Klingon territory. Their purpose was to expose Gowron, the Klingon leader, whom they suspected of being a changeling. However, it was General Martok, Gowron's right-hand man, who turned out to be the changeling in question.

Later on, Sisko and some of his officers came across a crashed Jem'Hadar warship while exploring a world in the Gamma Quadrant. When another Jem'Hadar ship showed up, Sisko and his enemies contended for the vessel—but neither side got what it wanted from it.

After learning that Cardassia had joined the Dominion, Sisko was forced to deal with what appeared to be a devastating assault force made up of cloaked Jem'Hadar and Cardassian warships. However, the attack turned out to be a ruse to conceal a more insidious plot—to transform Bajor's sun into a supernova, destroying Bajor and *Deep Space Nine* in the process.

Sisko was sometimes forced to join forces with his enemies. In 2372, he succeeded in stopping a group of Jem'Hadar renegades from gaining immense power by working alongside a sanctioned group of Jem'Hadar. Though the captain saved the life of the Jem'Hadar leader with whom he was aligned, the Jem'Hadar threatened to kill Sisko next time they met.

The captain also found it necessary to ally himself with the Cardassians on occasion. In one such instance, Thomas Riker—a duplicate of the *Enterprise*-D's Will Riker—stole the *Defiant* on behalf of the Maquis. Concerned that the Cardassians would believe the Federation had made an alliance with the Maquis, Sisko was forced to help his Cardassian nemesis, Gul Dukat, find and destroy the *Defiant*. In the end, Sisko was able to negotiate a deal to retrieve his ship and preserve Thomas Riker's life.

On another occasion, when the Klingons invaded Cardassia, Sisko deemed it necessary to warn the Cardassians and even do battle with the Klingons. Eventually, the captain was able to convince Gowron, the leader of the Klingon High Council, that a split among the Federation, the Klingons, and the Cardassians was just what the Dominion wanted to see.

Officer and Emissary

Though skeptical of his role as the Bajoran Emissary, the captain gradually came to embrace it, seeing the potential for doing good it brought him. A key point in this process was an incident in 2371, in which Sisko ignored an ancient Bajoran prophecy of doom to undertake a joint scientific venture with the Cardassians. When the prophecy came true, albeit in a symbolic way, Sisko developed a new respect for Bajoran mysticism—and for his own prophesied part in Bajor's fate.

A year later, Akorem Laan, a legendary Bajoran poet who had vanished into the wormhole two hundred years earlier, claimed that *he* was the Emissary. Sisko stepped aside without argument to let Akorem assume the position—until he saw the misery caused by Akorem's reverence for Bajor's ancient caste system. In the end, the wormhole aliens known as the Prophets confirmed that Sisko was the true Emissary.

In 2373, Sisko was plagued by life-threatening visions that enabled him to find B'hala, Bajor's legendary lost city, which seemed to hold the key to Bajor's future. When his life was saved by the station's physician, Dr. Julian Bashir, the visions went away—and the captain felt the loss deeply.

That same year, Sisko and some of his officers traveled back in time to a pivotal moment in the history of the original *Starship Enterprise*. Arne Darvin, a surgically altered Klingon, had used a Bajoran orb to send the *Defiant* back into the past, aiming to kill Captain James Kirk and alter history in his favor. Rubbing elbows with Kirk and his legendary crew, Sisko and his people managed to foil Darvin's plot and preserve the timeline.

One of Sisko's favorite recreational activities was a holosuite program of the pastime known as "baseball," in which he was able to pit his skills against the sport's greatest players—including Buck Bokai, Tris Speaker, and Ted Williams. Using this program, Sisko was able to teach his son, Jake, how to play the game. The program also allowed him to cheer his hero, Buck Bokai, in the sparsely attended 2042 World Series that heralded the end of professional baseball.

Sisko was an aficionado of other aspects of twenty-first-century Earth history as well. This interest stood him in good stead when he and Dr. Bashir were transported to the San Francisco of 2024—the time and place of the infamous Bell riots.

The captain enjoyed collecting ancient African artifacts. In fact, he tried to bring one back with him every time he visited Earth.

One of Sisko's most remarkable recreational activities was his construction of a Bajoran solar-sail vessel of ancient design, which he completed in 2371. Along with his son, Jake, Sisko piloted the vessel to Cardassia, dramatically demonstrating how ancient Bajorans might have accomplished the same feat some eight centuries earlier.

Sisko had a "problem" with losing, as evidenced by his preoccupation with the Maquis leader Michael Eddington. Eddington had served aboard *Deep Space Nine* for eighteen months as Starfleet security officer before showing his true colors as a rebel. Taking the deception personally, Sisko finally apprehended Eddington by casting himself as the villain of the piece and appealing to the rebel's penchant for self-sacrifice.

Despite his soft-spoken and often charming demeanor, no Starfleet officer has ever been as strong-willed, as tough, or as downright courageous as the estimable Benjamin Sisko.

Look for STAR TREK Fiction from Pocket Books

Star Trek®: The Original Series

Star Trek: The Motion Picture • Gene Roddenberry
Star Trek II: The Wrath of Khan • Vonda N. McIntyre
Star Trek III: The Search for Spock • Vonda N. McIntyre
Star Trek IV: The Voyage Home • Vonda N. McIntyre
Star Trek V: The Final Frontier • J. M. Dillard
Star Trek VI: The Undiscovered Country • J. M. Dillard
Star Trek VII: Generations • J. M. Dillard
Enterprise: The First Adventure • Vonda N. McIntyre
Final Frontier • Diane Carey
Strangers from the Sky • Margaret Wander Bonanno
Spock's World • Diane Duane
The Lost Years • J. M. Dillard
Probe • Margaret Wander Bonanno
Prime Directive • Judith and Garfield Reeves-Stevens
Best Destiny • Diane Carey
Shadows on the Sun • Michael Jan Friedman
Sarek • A. C. Crispin
Federation • Judith and Garfield Reeves-Stevens
The Ashes of Eden • William Shatner & Judith and Garfield
    Reeves-Stevens
The Return • William Shatner & Judith and Garfield Reeves-
    Stevens
Star Trek: Starfleet Academy • Diane Carey
Vulcan's Forge • Josepha Sherman and Susan Shwartz
Avenger • William Shatner & Judith and Garfield Reeves-Stevens

#1 *Star Trek: The Motion Picture* • Gene Roddenberry
#2 *The Entropy Effect* • Vonda N. McIntyre
#3 *The Klingon Gambit* • Robert E. Vardeman
#4 *The Covenant of the Crown* • Howard Weinstein
#5 *The Prometheus Design* • Sondra Marshak & Myrna
    Culbreath
#6 *The Abode of Life* • Lee Correy
#7 *Star Trek II: The Wrath of Khan* • Vonda N. McIntyre
#8 *Black Fire* • Sonni Cooper
#9 *Triangle* • Sondra Marshak & Myrna Culbreath
#10 *Web of the Romulans* • M. S. Murdock

Star Trek: The Next Generation®

Star Trek: Deep Space Nine®

Star Trek®: Voyager™

Flashback • Diane Carey
The Black Shore • Greg Cox
Mosaic • Jeri Taylor

#1 *Caretaker* • L. A. Graf
#2 *The Escape* • Dean W. Smith & Kristine K. Rusch
#3 *Ragnarok* • Nathan Archer
#4 *Violations* • Susan Wright
#5 *Incident at Arbuk* • John Greggory Betancourt
#6 *The Murdered Sun* • Christie Golden
#7 *Ghost of a Chance* • Mark A. Garland & Charles G.
     McGraw
#8 *Cybersong* • S. N. Lewitt
#9 *Invasion #4: The Final Fury* • Dafydd ab Hugh
#10 *Bless the Beasts* • Karen Haber
#11 *The Garden* • Melissa Scott
#12 *Chrysalis* • David Niall Wilson
#13 *The Black Shore* • Greg Cox
#14 *Marooned* • Christie Golden
#15 *Echoes* • Dean W. Smith & Kristine K. Rusch

Star Trek®: New Frontier

#1 *House of Cards* • Peter David
#2 *Into the Void* • Peter David
#3 *The Two-Front War* • Peter David
#4 *End Game* • Peter David
#5 *Martyr* • Peter David
#6 *Fire on High* • Peter David

Star Trek®: Day of Honor

Book One: *Ancient Blood* • Diane Carey
Book Two: *Armageddon Sky* • L. A. Graf
Book Three: *Her Klingon Soul* • Michael Jan Friedman
Book Four: *Treaty's Law* • Dean W. Smith & Kristine K. Rusch

Star Trek®: The Captain's Table